CREEPYPASTA:
BLACKEDITION

These stories are works of fiction. If you believe they are real you are terribly misunderstood. Credits to the authors of these stories are included before each story, a total of 16. If there is no credit, I wasn't provided with one. I have not written any of these stories because I am not that good of a writer. Have fun! And don't die! Oh and one more thing. You may be wondering, "What's a creepypasta?"Well reader of this compilation of stories, a creepypasta is a short "campfire story "written on the internet to scare the reader. Why do they call it that? Don't ask me. Oh and some stories that have no credit, I will give credit to the person who made the picture.

I got the stories from these websites:

Copyright www.creepypasta.wikia.com
©2014

Copyright www.creepypasta.com
©2014

Mason

By melissaurus

It was a dark and rainy day in February when I was hit by a small red pickup. February 15th. I was told I flew 15 feet before landing smack on my head. Apparently the driver was drunk and didn't see me crossing.

I don't remember that day at all.

Four weeks I slept, in a coma that many feared I would never come out of. I was placed in a ward of children and teens with major bodily harm or disease. My roommate was a boy named Mason. I never did find out his last name. For the time in which I slept, he found out bits and pieces of me from my various visitors. My favourite colour, what music I liked, and other random things.

The day I woke up, I was showered with love and attention from my family and it took me almost an hour to realise the presence of the boy laying in the bed beside me. He flashed me a lopsided grin and quietly went back to the book he was reading.

Eventually I was left in peace and after about 20 minutes of mental debate, I spoke up and asked him his name. His voice was smooth and low and never failed to make me shudder. We spent the rest of the evening playing 20 questions and becoming familiar with each other.

Eventually, my doctor would break our quality time and give me the low down on my injuries and what the healing process would be like. He told me that when I was hit, not only did I give myself a nasty concussion, but my legs were also broken in my oh so gracefully landing.

They said I had a 60% chance of ever walking again.

We became close instantaneously. The nurses would laugh and say we already looked like an old married couple bundled up in bed watching whatever soap opera happened to be on television. Mason would just flash me his trademark grin while I blushed and buried my face in his chest.

We both had our good days and bad ones, Mason and I. On a particularly tough day of treatment for him, we both lay together with him trembling in my arms. I'll never forget the feeling of his soft hiccups or the knot at the pit of my stomach. I finally got up my courage and asked him the million dollar question.

He had Hodgkin's disease. I don't think either of us slept that night.

While my legs were transitioned from casts to braces, Mason's chemotherapy began. However, without fail, when I'd come back frustrated or in tears over a difficult session of therapy, he'd be there to comfort me with soothing words and reruns of I Love Lucy.

Over the weeks, the chemo began to take it's toll. His brown curls thinned to almost nothing, dark circles took permanent residence under his eyes, and his skin turned as pale as snow. As my legs grew stronger, the day I was released no longer seemed like something to look forward to.

The day we decided to shave his hair was the day I broke down. I told him I would do anything; give blood, bone marrow, anything to make him get better faster, but he just shot me his smile that instantly made me melt and wiped my tears away.

60%. Mason had a sixty percent chance of beating his demons. Same as me.

On May 12, I was officially released from room 104. I would walk with a limp most likely for the rest of my life. Every other day I would visit Mason. Each time I would leave we would take a picture together. Over the months I could compare our first picture and our most recent one and see how much he was deteriorating. It was heartbreaking.

August 17 was the first time I lost him. Overnight a high fever had broken out and his heart stopped for 4 1/2 minutes. Those were the worst minutes of my life. I sat outside his room in an uncomfortable plastic chair watching the nurses I knew all too well scrambling back and forth attempting to save his fragile life.

I didn't leave his side until he squeezed my hand, winked, and told me to go home and take a shower.

After that, I vowed I would never let him leave me alone again.

I guess the odds weren't in Mason's favour for by the time Thanksgiving came around, he was almost a skeleton. But I didn't care.

He confided in me that night, accepting the fact that his time was almost up and promising to wait for me on the other side. I begged him not to go, but he just lightly shook his head and rubbed soft circles into my back. He wasn't going to survive to see Christmas.

That was two months ago.

No longer being able to bear to see him hooked up to all sorts of machines, we decided to steal away in the night together. I bundled him up and we drove away in my mother's car until we arrived at an old cabin my family would stay in during the holidays. Mason and I couldn't be any happier. I don't care that I'm on the news every night, or that every cop in the county is looking for me.

All I care about is being with Mason forever.

Even if his flesh is crawling with maggots and beginning to peel off his bones. Even if the smell off his rotting cadaver never fades from my skin. His lips are still warm at night and he often whispers sweet secrets into my ear before we sleep. No one, not the police, doctors, or anyone else can ever separate us. I'm ready for them when they come.

I made sure to bring the sharpest scalpel I could find when we left the hospital.

But until then, I'll lay in Mason's arms, or at least what I think were once his strong appendages, and we'll talk all night until he takes me away.

We'll be together forever.

Jeff the Killer

By ClericofMadness

Excerpt from a local Newspaper:

OMINOUS UNKNOWN
KILLER IS STILL
AT LARGE.

After weeks of unexplained murders, the ominous unknown killer is still on the rise. After little evidence has been found, a young boy states that he survived one of the killer's attacks and bravely tells his story.

"I had a bad dream and I woke up in the middle of the night," says the boy, "I saw that for some reason the window was open, even though I remember it being closed before I went to bed. I got up and shut it once more. Afterwards, I simply crawled under my covers and tried to get back to sleep. That's when I had a strange feeling, like someone was watching me. I looked up, and nearly jumped out of my bed. There, in the little ray of light, illuminating from between my curtains, were a pair of two eyes. These weren't regular eyes; they were dark, ominous eyes. They were bordered in black and... just plain out terrified me. That's when I saw his mouth. A long, horrendous smile that made every hair on my body stand up. The figure stood there, watching me. Finally, after what seemed like forever, he said it. A simple phrase, but said in a way only a mad man could speak.

"He said, 'Go To Sleep.' I let out a scream, that's what sent him at me. He pulled up a knife; aiming at my heart. He jumped on top of my bed. I fought him back; I kicked, I punched, I rolled around, trying to knock him off me. That's when my dad busted in. The man threw the knife, it went into my dad's shoulder. The man probably would've finished him off, if one of the neighbors hadn't alerted the police.

"They drove into the parking lot, and ran towards the door. The man turned and ran down the hallway. I heard a smash, like glass breaking. As I came out of my room, I saw the window that was pointing towards the back of my house was broken. I looked out it to see him vanish into the distance. I can tell you one thing, I will never forget that face. Those cold, evil eyes, and that psychotic smile. They will never leave my head."

Police are still on the look for this man. If you see anyone that fits the description in this story, please contact your local police department.

Jeff and his family had just moved into a new neighborhood. His dad had gotten a promotion at work, and they thought it would be best to live in one of those "fancy" neighborhoods. Jeff and his brother Liu couldn't complain though. A new, better house. What was not to love? As they were getting unpacked, one of their neighbors came by.

"Hello," she said, "I'm Barbara; I live across the street from you. Well, I just wanted to introduce myself and to introduce my son." She turns around and calls her son over. "Billy, these are our new neighbors." Billy said hi and ran back to play in his yard.

"Well," said Jeff's mom, "I'm Margaret, and this is my husband Peter, and my two sons, Jeff and Liu." They each introduced themselves, and then Barbara invited them to her son's birthday. Jeff and his brother were about to object, when their mother said that they would love to. When Jeff and his family are done packing, Jeff went up to his mom.

"Mom, why would you invite us to some kid's party? If you haven't noticed, I'm not some dumb kid."

"Jeff," said his mother, "We just moved here; we should show that we want to spend time with our neighbors. Now, we're going to that party, and that's final." Jeff started to talk, but stopped himself, knowing that he couldn't do anything. Whenever his mom said something, it was final. He walked up to his room and plopped down on his bed. He sat there looking at his ceiling when suddenly, he got a weird feeling. Not so much a pain, but... a weird feeling. He dismissed it as just some random feeling. He heard his mother call him down to get his stuff, and he walked down to get it.

The next day, Jeff walked down stairs to get breakfast and got ready for school. As he sat there, eating his breakfast, he once again got that feeling. This time it was stronger. It gave him a slight tugging pain, but he once again dismissed it. As he and Liu finished breakfast, they walked down to the bus stop. They sat there waiting for the bus, and then, all of a sudden, some kid on a skateboard jumped over them, only inches above their laps. They both jumped back in surprise. "Hey, what the hell?"

The kid landed and turned back to them. He kicked his skate board up and caught it with his hands. The kid seems to be about twelve; one year younger than Jeff. He wears an Aeropostale shirt and ripped blue jeans.

"Well, well, well. It looks like we got some new meat." Suddenly, two other kids appeared. One was super skinny and the other was huge. "Well, since you're new here, I'd like to introduce ourselves, over there is Keith." Jeff and Liu looked over to the skinny kid. He had a dopey face that you would expect a sidekick to have. "And he's Troy." They looked over at the fat kid. Talk about a tub of lard. This kid looked like he hadn't exercised since he was crawling.

"And I," said the first kid, "am Randy. Now, for all the kids in this neighborhood there is a small price for bus fare, if you catch my drift." Liu stood up, ready to punch the lights out of the kid's eyes when one of his friends pulled a knife on him. "Tsk, tsk, tsk, I had hoped you would be more cooperative, but it seems we must do this the hard way." The kid walked up to Liu and took his wallet out of his pocket. Jeff got that feeling again. Now, it was truly strong; a burning sensation. He stood up, but Liu gestured him to sit down. Jeff ignored him and walked up to the kid.

"Listen here you little punk, give back my bro's wallet or else." Randy put the wallet in his pocket and pulled out his own knife.

"Oh? And what will you do?" Just as he finished the sentence, Jeff popped the kid in the nose. As Randy reached for his face, Jeff grabbed the kid's wrist and broke it. Randy screamed and Jeff grabbed the knife from his hand. Troy and Keith rushed Jeff, but Jeff was too quick. He threw Randy to the ground. Keith lashed out at him, but Jeff ducked and stabbed him in the arm. Keith dropped his knife and fell to the ground screaming. Troy rushed him too, but Jeff didn't even need the knife. He just punched Troy straight in the stomach and Troy went down. As he fell, he puked all over. Liu could do nothing but look in amazement at Jeff.

"Jeff how'd you?" that was all he said. They saw the bus coming and knew they'd be blamed for the whole thing. So they started running as fast as they could. As they ran, they looked back and saw the bus driver rushing over to Randy and the others. As Jeff and Liu made it to school, they didn't dare tell what happened. All they did was sit and listen. Liu just thought of that as his brother beating up a few kids, but Jeff knew it was more. It was something, scary. As he got that feeling he felt how powerful it was, the urge to just, hurt someone. He didn't like how it sounded, but he couldn't help feeling happy. He felt that strange feeling go away, and stay away for the entire day of school. Even as he walked home due to the whole thing near the bus stop, and how now he probably wouldn't be taking the bus anymore, he felt happy. When he got home his parents asked him how his day was, and he said, in a somewhat ominous voice, "It was a wonderful day." Next morning, he heard a knock at his front door. He walked down to find two police officers at the door, his mother looking back at him with an angry look.

"Jeff, these officers tell me that you attacked three kids. That it wasn't regular fighting, and that they were stabbed.

Stabbed, son!" Jeff's gaze fell to the floor, showing his mother that it was true.

"Mom, they were the ones who pulled the knives on me and Liu."

"Son," said one of the cops," We found three kids, two stabbed, one having a bruise on his stomach, and we have witnesses proving that you fled the scene. Now, what does that tell us?" Jeff knew it was no use. He could say him and Liu had been attacked, but then there was no proof it was not them who attacked first. They couldn't say that they weren't fleeing, because truth be told they were. So Jeff couldn't defend himself or Liu.

"Son, call down your brother." Jeff couldn't do it, since it was him who beat up all the kids.

"Sir, it...it was me. I was the one who beat up the kids. Liu tried to hold me back, but he couldn't stop me." The cop looked at his partner and they both nod.

"Well kid, looks like a year in Juvy..."

"Wait!" says Liu. They all looked up to see him holding a knife. The officers pulled their guns and locked them on Liu.

"It was me, I beat up those little punks. Have the marks to prove it." He lifted up his sleeves to reveal cuts and bruises, as if he was in a struggle.

"Son, just put the knife down," said the officer. Liu held up the knife and dropped it to the ground. He put his hands up and walked over to the cops.

"No Liu, it was me! I did it!" Jeff had tears running down his face.

"Huh, poor bro. Trying to take the blame for what I did. Well, take me away." The police led Liu out to the patrol car.

"Liu, tell them it was me! Tell them! I was the one who beat up those kids!" Jeff's mother put her hands on his shoulders.

"Jeff please, you don't have to lie. We know it's Liu, you can stop." Jeff watched helplessly as the cop car speeds off with Liu inside. A few minutes later Jeff's dad pulled into the driveway, seeing Jeff's face and knowing something was wrong.

"Son, son what is it?" Jeff couldn't answer. His vocal cords were strained from crying. Instead, Jeff's mother walked his father inside to break the bad news to him as Jeff wept in the driveway. After an hour or so Jeff walked back in to the house, seeing that his parents were both shocked, sad, and disappointed. He couldn't look at them. He couldn't see how they thought of Liu when it was his fault. He just went to sleep, trying to get the whole thing off his mind. Two days went by, with no word from Liu at JDC. No friends to hang out with. Nothing but sadness and guilt. That is until Saturday, when Jeff is woke up by his mother, with a happy, sunshiny face.

"Jeff, it's the day." she said as she opened up the curtains and let light flood into his room.

"What, what's today?" asked Jeff as he stirs awake.

"Why, it's Billy's party." He was now fully awake.

"Mom, you're joking, right? You don't expect me to go to some kid's party after..." There was a long pause.

"Jeff, we both know what happened. I think this party could be the thing that brightens up the past days. Now, get dressed." Jeff's mother walked out of the room and downstairs to get ready herself. He fought himself to get up. He picked out a random shirt and pair of jeans and walked down stairs. He saw his mother and father all dressed up; his mother in a dress and his father in a suit. He thought, why they would ever wear such fancy clothes to a kid's party?

"Son, is that all you're going to wear?" said Jeff's mom.

"Better than wearing too much." he said. His mother pushed down the feeling to yell at him and hid it with a smile.

"Now Jeff, we may be over-dressed, but this is how you go if you want to make an impression." said his father. Jeff grunted and went back up to his room.

"I don't have any fancy clothes!" he yelled down stairs.

"Just pick out something." called his mother. He looked around in his closet for what he would call fancy. He found a pair of black dress pants he had for special occasions and an undershirt. He couldn't find a shirt to go with it though. He looked around, and found only striped and patterned shirts. None of which go with dress pants. Finally he found a white hoodie and put it on.

"You're wearing that?" they both said. His mother looked at her watch. "Oh, no time to change. Let's just go." She said as she herded Jeff and his father out the door. They crossed the street over to Barbara and Billy's house. They knocked on the door and at it appeared that Barbara, just like his parents, way over-dressed. As they walked inside all Jeff could see were adults, no kids.

"The kids are out in the yard. Jeff, how about you go and meet some of them?" said Barbara.

Jeff walked outside to a yard full of kids. They were running around in weird cowboy costumes and shooting each other with plastic guns. He might as well be standing in a Toys R Us. Suddenly a kid came up to him and handed him a toy gun and hat.

"Hey. Wanna pway?" he said.

"Ah, no kid. I'm way too old for this stuff." The kid looked at him with that weird puppy dog face.

"Pwease?" said the kid. "Fine," said Jeff. He put on the hat and started to pretend shoot at the kids. At first he thought it was totally ridiculous, but then he started to actually have fun. It might not have been super cool, but it was the first time he had done something that took his mind off of Liu. So he played with the kids for a while, until he heard a noise. A weird rolling noise. Then it hit him. Randy, Troy, and Keith all jumped over the fence on their skateboards. Jeff dropped the fake gun and ripped off the hat. Randy looked at Jeff with a burning hatred.

"Hello, Jeff, is it?" he said. "We have some unfinished business." Jeff saw his bruised nose." I think we're even. I beat the crap out of you, and you get my brother sent to JDC."

Randy got an angry look in his eyes. "Oh no, I don't go for even, I go for winning. You may have kicked our asses that one day, but not today." As he said that Randy rushed at Jeff. They both fell to the ground. Randy punched Jeff in the nose, and Jeff grabbed him by the ears and head butted him. Jeff pushed Randy off of him and both rose to their feet. Kids were screaming and parents were running out of the house. Troy and Keith both pulled guns out of their pockets.

"No one interrupts or guts will fly!" they said. Randy pulled a knife on Jeff and stabbed it into his shoulder.

Jeff screamed and fell to his knees. Randy started kicking him in the face. After three kicks Jeff grabs his foot and twists it, causing Randy to fall to the ground. Jeff stood up and walked towards the back door. Troy grabbed him.

"Need some help?" He picks Jeff up by the back of the collar and throws him through the patio door. As Jeff tries to stand he is kicked down to the ground. Randy repeatedly starts kicking Jeff, until he starts to cough up blood.

"Come on Jeff, fight me!" He picks Jeff up and throws him into the kitchen. Randy sees a bottle of vodka on the counter and smashes the glass over Jeff's head.

"Fight!" He throws Jeff back into the living room.

"Come on Jeff, look at me!" Jeff glances up, his face riddled with blood. "I was the one who got your brother sent to JDC! And now you're just gonna sit here and let him rot in there for a whole year! You should be ashamed!" Jeff starts to get up.

"Oh, finally! You stand and fight!" Jeff is now to his feet, blood and vodka on his face. Once again he gets that strange feeling, the one in which he hasn't felt for a while. "Finally. He's up!" says Randy as he runs at Jeff. That's when it happens. Something inside Jeff snaps. His psyche is destroyed, all rational thinking is gone, all he can do, is kill. He grabs Randy and pile drives him to the ground. He gets on top of him and punches him straight in the heart. The punch causes Randy's heart to stop. As Randy gasps for breath. Jeff hammers down on him. Punch after punch, blood gushes from Randy's body, until he takes one final breath, and dies.

Everyone is looking at Jeff now. The parents, the crying kids, even Troy and Keith. Although they easily break from their gaze and point their guns at Jeff. Jeff see's the guns trained on him and runs for the stairs. As he runs Troy and Keith let out fire on him, each shot missing. Jeff runs up the stairs. He hears Troy and Keith follow up behind. As they let out their final rounds of bullets Jeff ducks into the bathroom. He grabs the towel rack and rips it off the wall. Troy and Keith race in, knives ready.

Troy swings his knife at Jeff, who backs away and bangs the towel rack into Troy's face. Troy goes down hard and now all that's left is Keith. He is more agile than Troy though, and ducks when Jeff swings the towel rack. He dropped the knife and grabbed Jeff by the neck. He pushed him into the wall. A thing of bleach fell down on top of him from the top shelf. It burnt both of them and they both started to scream. Jeff wiped his eyes as best as he could. He pulled back the towel rack and swung it straight into Keith's head. As he lay there, bleeding to death, he let out an ominous smile.

"What's so funny?" asked Jeff. Keith pulled out a lighter and switched it on. "What's funny," he said, "Is that you're covered in bleach and alcohol." Jeff's eyes widened as Keith threw the lighter at him. As soon as the flame made contact with him, the flames ignited the alcohol in the vodka. While the alcohol burned him, the bleach bleached his skin. Jeff let out a terrible screech as he caught on fire. He tried to roll out the fire but it was no use, the alcohol had made him a walking inferno. He ran down the hall, and fell down the stairs. Everybody started screaming as they saw Jeff, now a man on fire, drop to the ground, nearly dead. The last thing Jeff saw was his mother and the other parents trying to extinguish the flame. That's when he passed out.

When Jeff woke he had a cast wrapped around his face. He couldn't see anything, but he felt a cast on his shoulder, and stitches all over his body. He tried to stand up, but he realized that there was some tube in his arm, and when he tried to get up it fell out, and a nurse rushed in.

"I don't think you can get out of bed just yet." she said as she put him back in his bed and re-inserted the tube. Jeff sat there, with no vision, no idea of what his surroundings were. Finally, after hours, he heard his mother.

"Honey, are you okay?" she asked. Jeff couldn't answer though, his face was covered, and he was unable to speak. "Oh honey, I have great news. After all the witnesses told the police that Randy confessed of trying to attack you, they decided to let Liu go." This made Jeff almost bolt up, stopping halfway, remembering the tube coming out of his arm. "He'll be out by tomorrow, and then you two will be able to be together again."

Jeff's mother hugs Jeff and says her goodbyes. The next couple of weeks were those where Jeff was visited by his family. Then came the day where his bandages were to be removed. His family were all there to see it, what he would look like. As the doctors unwrapped the bandages from Jeff's face everyone was on the edge of their seats. They waited until the last bandage holding the cover over his face was almost removed.

"Let's hope for the best," said the doctor. He quickly pulls the cloth; letting the rest fall from Jeff's face.

Jeff's mother screams at the sight of his face. Liu and Jeff's dad stare awe-struck at his face.

"What? What happened to my face?" Jeff said. He rushed out of bed and ran to the bathroom. He looked in the mirror and saw the cause of the distress. His face. It... it's horrible. His lips were burnt to a deep shade of red. His face was turned into a pure white color, and his hair singed from brown to black. He slowly put his hand to his face. It had a sort of leathery feel to it now. He looked back at his family then back at the mirror.

"Jeff," said Liu, "It's not that bad..."

"Not that bad?" said Jeff," It's perfect!" His family were equally surprised. Jeff started laughing uncontrollably His parents noticed that his left eye and hand were twitching.

"Uh... Jeff, are you okay?"

"Okay? I've never felt happier! Ha ha ha ha ha haaaaaa, look at me. This face goes perfectly with me!" He couldn't stop laughing. He stroked his face feeling it. Looking at it in the mirror. What caused this? Well, you may recall that when Jeff was fighting Randy something in his mind, his sanity, snapped. Now he was left as a crazy killing machine, that is, his parents didn't know.

"Doctor," said Jeff's mom, "Is my son... alright, you know. In the head?"

"Oh yes, this behavior is typical for patients that have taken very large amounts of pain killers. If his behavior doesn't change in a few weeks, bring him back here, and we'll give him a psychological test."

"Oh thank you doctor." Jeff's mother went over to Jeff." Jeff, sweety. It's time to go."

Jeff looks away from the mirror, his face still formed into a crazy smile. "Kay mommy, ha ha haaaaaaaaaaaaa!" his mother took him by the shoulder and took him to get his clothes.

"This is what came in," said the lady at the desk. Jeff's mom looked down to see the black dress pants and white hoodie her son wore. Now they were clean of blood and now stitched together. Jeff's mother led him to his room and made him put his clothes on. Then they left, not knowing that this was their final day of life.

Later that night, Jeff's mother woke to a sound coming from the bathroom. It sounded as if someone was crying. She slowly walked over to see what it was. When she looked into the bathroom she saw a horrendous sight. Jeff had taken a knife and carved a smile into his cheeks.

"Jeff, what are you doing?" asked his mother.

Jeff looked over to his mother. "I couldn't keep smiling mommy. It hurt after a while. Now, I can smile forever. Jeff's mother noticed his eyes, ringed in black.

"Jeff, your eyes!" His eyes were seemingly never closing.

"I couldn't see my face. I got tired and my eyes started to close. I burned out the eyelids so I could forever see myself; my new face." Jeff's mother slowly started to back away, seeing that her son was going insane. "What's wrong mommy? Aren't I beautiful?

"Yes son," she said, "Yes you are. L-let me go get daddy, so he can see your face." She ran into the room and shook Jeff's dad from his sleep. "Honey, get the gun we..." She stopped as she saw Jeff in the doorway, holding a knife.

"Mommy, you lied." That's the last thing they hear as Jeff rushes them with the knife, gutting both of them.

His brother Liu woke up, startled by some noise. He didn't hear anything else, so he just shut his eyes and tried to go back to sleep. As he was on the border of slumber, he got the strangest feeling that someone was watching him. He looked up, before Jeff's hand covered his mouth. He slowly raised the knife ready to plunge it into Liu. Liu thrashed here and there trying to escape Jeff's grip.

"Shhhhhhh," Jeff said. "Just go to sleep."

Slenderman

By unknown

After waking up with a jolt, the girl laid in bed a few seconds longer. Reaching over to switch on her bedside lamp, she tried to remember exactly what had stolen her sweet slumber away. When she couldn't, the brunette swung her legs over the side of the bed and heaved herself up. Checking the time on her phone, she snorted when she saw it was midnight- the witching hour. Knowing that sleep would only evade her, she left her bedroom for the kitchen, a good cup of coffee on her mind.

As she passed by her front door, a chill spread like liquid fire down her spine. It's only winter, she told herself, focusing again on the coffee plan. Measuring out scoops, water, and preparing her cup kept her occupied, but as the dark liquid boiled, she had nothing left to keep her mind from wandering off. The chill returned and she couldn't help but glance behind her to the front door. It stood there innocently enough, just like always. The dead bolt was still in place and she could see nothing amiss with it. Turning back to her coffee, she did her best to forget about the feeling.

With her cup in hand, she started back towards her bedroom. As she walked by the front door, she decided that a quick glance out of the peep hole would help calm her restless mind. The chill worsened with each step she took towards the door and further away from the safety and warmth of her blankets. She pressed her empty hand against the cold, metal door and took a deep breath before leading her eye to the peep hole.

At first, she could only see an inky blackness and somehow seemed to swirl in itself. When she blinked in surprise, the void melted away. She wished it hadn't. In its place, there stood what she could only guess was once a man. The limbs were long and inhumanly awkward, with bulky joints branching off into several arms, not unlike the branches of a tree. The creature was draped in a black suit, somehow making the thing more nightmarish to her. The icing on the proverbial cake, however, was what passed as the hellish thing's face. It was as though her mind blurred the ghastly visage to spare itself further shock and horror.

She shoved herself away from the door with the hand still pressed against it. The scalding mug of coffee fell, the liquid burning her bare legs as she fell backwards and tried to crawl away from the door. She knew, somehow, that her mind hadn't been playing tricks on her. As she crab walked away from the door, she watched as tendrils as black as the void she first saw snake around through the cracks. The girl was trapped between the instinct to flee and the gut feeling to not turn her back on the door. When the door jolted, the urge to flee overcame her and she slipped in the burning liquid as she tried to make it back to her room.

She knew deep down that she was trapping herself in a corner, but she had to get away from the door. The girl was halfway down the hallway when she heard the previously locked door creak open. She screamed and slipped into a wall, cracking her chin on it and stunning her.

After that, there was only blackness.

—

"Nicole?" a warm, male voice snapped the woman out of her trance. As she turned around, she was met by one of her sister's doctor's. She nodded, not sure if she should say anything, or even if she could find her voice if she did have something to say. That morning, she had gotten an urgent phone call from the hospital, saying that her sister, Lindsay, was there. Before they had even let her see her, the doctor's had pulled her off to the side and insisted that they talk to her about what might have happened. Phrases like 'self-inflected' and 'assault' had been thrown around and Nicole felt her mind reel.

She still hadn't fully understood what they had been saying until she saw Lindsay with her own eyes. Her little sister had a bandage wrapped around her head, covering both of her ears as well as her eyes. They said it was to keep her now deadened eyes from drying out and to try to keep infection out of the wounds Lindsay had made to her ears. The doctors had guessed that either she or someone else had jammed a pencil into them to keep her off balance or to deafen herself against something. There was the mix of first and second degree burns on her hands, legs, and feet, from what was assumed to be the coffee her neighbors found slipped all over the entry to her apartment.

As Nicole walked into her sister's hospital room the first time, she thought she had spied the silhouette of a man in the window. That, she knew, was impossible. Her sister's room was on the third story of the hospital.

Case File No.57 (Stitch)
By Fear_of

I came home from the Christmas party unwillingly. I would've stayed at Anna's, but her parents were in town. My little apartment was not nearly as welcoming as it used to be, in the days before this Stitch creature came around. I keep thinking I'm hearing thumping, or windows opening, and it's freaking me out. But I came home anyway.

Maybe I just needed a break from the case. Yeah. For Sunday, Monday, and Tuesday I didn't touch those boxes once. The Boss handed me a couple cases of convenience store robberies that were easier to solve than a game of Clue.

It was a nice distraction from all the gruesome imagery I'd been forced to see those past few days. But unfortunately Wednesday had to come and Anna wanted to work on the case. "The sooner we start working again, the sooner it'll be over." she said trying to convince me to work with her. I sighed and put the coffee I was drinking down on my desk. Anna had put all the second victim related evidence on a table in a conference room. It was the first victim's cousin, the man who'd stayed with her the night she was murdered, Bill.

I looked at the pictures of the crime scene first. He'd been killed in his room at the mental hospital we'd been holding him at. The scene was just as bloody as that of his cousins, if not more. The walls were covered in bloody hand prints and the bars on the windows weren't bent, meaning Stitch must've found another way into the building. There were two beds in the room, one for Bill and one for his roommate; both were messy and blood stained. The red stood out vividly on the pristine white sheets.

When I got to the pictures of his body, there was only half. His legs were lying on the floor, bones sticking out and sitting in a pool of his blood. His white hospital clothing was no longer white, but blood red, like Snow White's lips. My hands began shaking as I looked at more and more pictures of his mangled and missing body and the blood soaked room. I felt my heart beating faster, like I was panicking. I didn't know why though. Why should I panic? Stitch couldn't find me...

"So what do you think we should do? We don't really have any leads on who this guy is," Anna said, bringing me out of my terrified state. I pulled myself together so I wouldn't scare my partner.

"I don't know," I replied.

Honestly, I didn't want to keep working on this case. But what choice did I have? I couldn't just leave Anna to handle it by herself. I couldn't convince the Boss to let us do something else. When a case got to us, it was because no one else could handle it and solve it. We were the top... I guess that's what comes with being the best detectives in the office. Some detective I am though can't even look at the pictures without shaking. I've been having nightmares too...

"I was thinking maybe we could go interview the mental hospital staff who worked with Bill. We should probably go over the security tape footage and journal entries first though. Didn't they diagnose him as PTSD?" Anna said.

"Yeah. I only took two psychology classes in college, but I remember that with Post Traumatic Stress Disorder a lot of the times therapists will tell their patients to relive the event a lot of times, so it won't cause them that overbearing stress… So I imagine that's what his journal will be full of. Just retellings of the story to help ease his anxiety, but I dunno. We probably should look through it," I said. I secretly hoped she'd watch the videos on her own and let me deal with the journals. But knowing her, knowing our jobs, that wasn't likely.

"Do you want to look at videos or journals first?" she asked. I shrugged and took a gulp of my now cold coffee.

"Let's do this then," I said. God damn it, I thought to myself as she put the four discs into four DVD players. They were all different cameras from the same period of time. For a while we just fast forwarded. Bill stayed in his room, writing feverishly, while his fellow hospital patients wandered from room to room to common room. He only left when a nurse came to bring him to his therapy session with the leading psychiatrist of the hospital. As it started to get dark, the patients made their way to their rooms.

Bills roommate walked into their room. Bill was still writing in his journal with a painful expression on his face. His roommate looked at him concerned. There was no sound, but we saw him say something along the lines of

"Are you okay?" Bill looked over at him and told him to "Shut up before that thing found him too" or something. His roommate looked away and leaned against the wall his bed was against. He played with his thumbs for a while. Meanwhile, the nurses wandered the halls, locking doors for the night, making sure everything was okay.

After about twenty minutes of that, Bill and his roommate laid down for the night and fell asleep. It was dark and we couldn't see much. The camera started turning to static and the images on the screens kept becoming distorted. The screens all blacked out and we were waiting for anything to happen. When the image returned, Stitch was standing in the middle of the hallway. He trudged down the hallway, looking through every room's door window to see if Bill was there. While he systematically wandered the hall, Bill sprang to life and rushed from window to door and back again, looking for what woke him.

Stitch stopped looking for Bill and appeared to sniff the air. He took a couple big sniffs then turned his head. His face was looking towards the camera. You could see his teeth. His mouth wasn't fully closed. His teeth were vile. Black and yellow and green and every color that teeth shouldn't be. He opened his mouth and a little bit of blood fell out. He kept moving his head back and forth. As if he was listening for something.

He walked straight to Bills room with determination in his steps and opened the door without touching it. Bill screamed, waking up his roommate. Bill flipped over on his side springing off of his bed. He grabbed what turned out to be his writing pencil. The cameras began to turn to static and cut out again. We could see bits and pieces of what was happening – both of the roommates running around, Bills roommate eventually ran out of the room and Bill had stabbed Stitch in his back. We're not sure how, but Bills hand and the weapon just went straight through, pushing out darkened blood and random chunks onto the floor. It looked like he was struggling to get his arm back. As if his arm got stuck inside Stitch's body. Stitch grabbed him by the hair and whipped him with his rusty shackles, breaking his skin.

After that, Stitch just stood there. Standing over Bill. Maybe it made him feel powerful? Well, could he even feel emotion? I don't know. He stood above him while Bill screamed. I thought Stitch was raising his hand to strike or rip Bill's flesh, but he didn't. He rubbed his hands together, and then rubbed from his neck up to his face. And as fast as you could see a light turn on, his hand was on Bills face. He started rubbing it. Running his hand through his hair. Stitch started laughing at that point, and blood dripped on Bills face and clothes.

It was then Stitch decided to attack. He tore bits of skin off his poor body and ate them like he'd never eaten before. He broke his body in half, just tore it in half, with inhuman strength. The blood started to really poor then. As all of Bills blood and guts spilled onto the floor, Stitch squatted down and started running his fingers along the edge of Bills skin where he ripped him in half. Stitch began eating his insides all the while it appeared he was laughing - just as he did in the first murder.

Stitch stood up and, well, just stood there. He stood there facing the corner until the morning sun started to peak in through the bars on the windows. He was mumbling to himself but since there was no audio in the security cameras, we couldn't make out what he was saying without bringing in someone who could read lips.

I didn't hear Anna making any sounds. I wondered if I was the only one having a hard time with this case. I looked over and she was crying silently. I moved my chair and put my arm around her and rubbed her shoulder while we watched. I tried to hold myself together for her. The door to the conference room slammed open, nearly giving both of us heart attacks.

"Johnson, Reynolds. Have an intern," the Boss said, pushing a young man into the room. He left as soon as he'd come. We stood up. Anna wiped her eyes hastily and paused the videos.

"I'm Anna," she said. "This is Ryan. I'm sorry you had to come at this time. We're working on a pretty nasty case."

"Oh, I don't mind," he said. "It's bound to happen eventually, so I may as well get myself acquainted with murder. I'm John Freeman." He held his hand out to us and shook both our hands.

"I think we've looked at enough evidence for now, Ryan. Want to go to the mental hospital now?" I said.

"Sure," Anna said. We headed out the door, with our new intern at our heels. With his slightly unkempt blond hair and puppy-like blue eyes, he reminded me of a golden retriever. I felt bad ruining his innocence with this horrifying case. But that's just what happens when you get involved with Police work…

~~

We made our way to West Seattle Psychiatric Hospital. It looked less welcoming than a medical hospital, just because of what lied within its walls. John looked at it with hesitation. I pushed him forward. If he wanted to be a cop, he'd have to learn to deal with situations he didn't want to be in. And this case was about as bad as it gets, so if he could handle this, he could handle anything. We went into the building and found the nurses who were involved with Bill and his treatment. They wore white uniforms, like you saw in the movies and were as kind as you would expect nurses to be.

"Hi, Miss, I'm Ryan Johnson, this is my partner Anna Reynolds and our intern John Freeman. We're working on Bill and his cousin's case. We just have a few questions."

"Of course," the first nurse said, nodding with a smile.

"Did you notice anything out of the ordinary with Bills behavior before the attack? In the videos we saw him panicking moments before the killer came, but not before then. We don't know what was normal or abnormal in his condition," Anna asked.

"Well, he was always very agitated, always writing in his journal. The Doctor told him to write his story down at least once a day, but he did it almost constantly. We think maybe he was desperate to get better. Or get out. He kept saying he needed to keep moving or else 'that thing' as he called it would find him," the second nurse said. Anna wrote some notes down.

"But you didn't notice anything abnormal?" I asked again.

"No, sir, nothing. Just his usual behavior."

"Did you see anyone lurking around the building at all? Like before the attack or in the days preceding it?" I asked.

"No, sir. Or if the killer was here he was very good at hiding," the first nurse said.

"Did you see which way the killer went after the attack?" I asked. The nurses both became quiet and turned a little pale.

"No, sir," the first nurse said quietly. "We saw him throw part of Bill out the window and follow, but we didn't see which way he went once he was on the ground outside."

"Thank you for your help," I said, even though they really hadn't given us anything useful. They nodded.

"Of course, any time," the second nurse said. They turned around and continued with their work. We left in silence. Once we got into the car, I was irritated. How were we ever going to find this guy and put him behind bars (if that would even help…) if we couldn't find a single lead?

"This is just great," Anna said, sounding equally as frustrated. She sighed loudly.

"Let's just work on this some more tomorrow," I said. We drove back to the station. I got into my own car and drove back to my apartment reluctantly. Weird things had been happening ever since I first opened the boxes to this case. I kept hearing thumping at night and creaking like my windows were opening. But I wasn't sure if I was just hearing things or not. I could never find the sources of the sounds. I opened my apartment door half expecting Stitch to be waiting for me. I'd been becoming paranoid, scared. Just fact that I was becoming paranoid and scared was scaring me.

I walked into my apartment, finding no one inside. It was colder than I expected it to be. I wandered through all the rooms, only to find what I hoped I wouldn't. My bedroom window was opened. I swear I locked it before I left. My hands shook as I closed it and my heart started to race.

The panic was setting in again. I turned on all the lights in my apartment on my way to the kitchen to make some comfort food. I made a giant sandwich, grabbed a can of soda and some chips, and walked into the living room. Desperate to take my mind of that god awful case, I turned on the TV and put on a funny movie – Anchorman to be exact.

I always loved Will Ferrell. I ate my food and soon my mind was far from the case. Until I heard the thumping. Thump. Thump. Thump. Thump. It rang in my ears, echoed in my mind, until I couldn't take it. I ran to my bedroom and grabbed the ear plugs out of my bed side table. I shoved them into my ears to stop that thumping. My window was open again. I still heard the thumping. That god damn thumping. My heart was racing, my palms were sweating, and my hands were shaking so hard I could barely grab the phone. I dialed Anna's number as quickly as I could.

"He-" she started.

"Anna! Can I stay over tonight?" I asked, cutting her off.

"Sure, what's wrong, Ryan?" she asked.

"Please don't tell me I'm not the only one having problems with this case," I said, nearly begging.

"Are you freaking out too? I swear, I keep closing my windows, but they're always open…" she said, trailing off.

"I'll be over in ten minutes." I hung up the phone and packed a bag as quickly as I could.

~~

We both actually got sleep that night. We drove to work in our separate cars in case I decided to sleep at my own house that night. Neither of us wanted to dive back into the case, but instead of Anna making me, it was John making us. He reiterated almost exactly what Anna had said. "Come on, guys, the sooner we start working the sooner it'll be over!" He was annoyingly chipper all the time. But I was friendly, so was Anna. He put the tapes back in and pushed play. They started where we'd left off. John looked at them intently, taking notes about all the gruesome things Stitch was doing. I could hardly watch.

Stitch picked up Bills upper half like a bowling ball, sticking his fingers in Bills eyes and mouth. His hand was still embedded in Stitch's disgusting naked body as he dragged him out into the hall. A trail of blood followed the poor dead man's body. When Stitch reached the window, he tore Bills arm off and threw the rest of his body out the broken window. From the other angle, we could see Bills roommate still cowering in horror. Stitch ignored him and tore the arm from his chest.

Dark goo-like blood came out with the arm, leaving a gaping hole where there should be something…anything… He didn't even seem to care. He put Bills hand in his repulsive mouth and ate three of his fingers. I imagined the sound of crunching bones and shuddered. He smiles at the camera as he eats Bills remains. His teeth were rotten, his lips were still bleeding, his eyes still covered in sewn on flesh… The video cut out again and when the image returned, Stitch was gone and Bills arm was on the floor. His roommate was crying. I looked at Anna who looked back at me.

"Maybe you should just live with me for a while. I'm too scared to live alone," she said quietly. I was glad to know I wasn't the only one scared out of my wits. Maybe the two of us together would be enough to keep Stitch away. We'd start looking at victim number three soon. After we'd had some time to regain our sanity.

Laughing Jack
By SnuffBomb

It was a nice summer day, my 5-year-old son James was playing outside in the backyard of our suburban home. James has always been a quiet boy, he plays by himself mostly, he never had many friends, but he has always had a wild imagination. I was in the kitchen feeding our dog Fido, when I heard what sounded like James talking to someone in the backyard. I'm not sure who it was he could be talking to, could he have finally made a friend? Being a single mom it's hard for me to always keep an eye on my son, so I decided to go outside and check on him.

When I went into the backyard I was a bit confused, because James was the only person back there. Was he talking to himself? I could have sworn I heard another voice. "James! It's time to come inside." I called out to him. He came inside and sat down at the kitchen table, it was about lunchtime so I decided to make him a turkey sandwich. "James. Who were you talking to out there?" I asked. James looked up for a moment, "I was playing with my new friend," he said smiling. I poured him some milk and continued to pry, as any good mother would. "Does your friend have a name? Why didn't you ask him to have lunch with us?" I asked. James stared at me for a moment before replying, "His name is Laughing Jack." I was a bit taken back by what he had said. "Oh? That's a strange name. What does your friend look like?" I asked a bit confused. "He's a clown. He has long hair and a big swirly cone nose. He's got long arms and baggy pants, with stripy socks, and he always smiles." I realized my son was talking about an imaginary friend. I suppose it is normal for kids his age to have imaginary friends, especially when he has no real kids to play with. It's probably just a phase.

The rest of the day went by as per usual, and it was starting to get late so I put James to bed. I tucked him in, gave him a kiss, and made sure to turn on his nightlight before I closed the door. I was pretty tired myself so I decided to go to bed not long after. I had an awful nightmare…

It was dark. I was in some kind of rundown amusement park. I was scared, running through an endless field of empty tents, broken down rides, and abandoned game huts. The whole place had a horrible look to it. Everything was black and white, the prize stuffed animals all hung from nooses in the game huts, all with sick grins stitched on their faces. It felt like the whole park was looking at me, even though there wasn't another living thing in sight. Then suddenly, I began to hear music play. The sounds of Pop Goes the Weasel being played on a squeezebox echoed through the park, it was hypnotizing. I followed its tune to the circus tent almost in a trance, unable to stop my legs from moving forward. It was pitch black, the only light came from a single spotlight shining on the center of the big top. As I walked toward the light the music slowed down, I found myself singing along unable to stop.

"All around the mulberry bush

The monkey chased the weasel

The monkey though twas all in fun…"

The music stopped right before its climax, and suddenly the lights shot on. The intensity of the lights was practically blinding, all I could see was a small dark silhouette shuffle towards me. Then another one appeared, and another, and another. There were dozens of them, all coming toward me. I couldn't move, my legs were frozen, all I could do was watch as the haunting figures drew nearer. As they got closer I could see… THEY WERE CHILDREN! As I looked at each one I noticed they were all horribly disfigured and mutilated. Some had cuts all over their body, others were severely burnt, and others were missing limbs, even eyes! The children enveloped me, clawing at my flesh, dragging me to the ground, and tearing inside me. As the children tore me apart and I faded away, all I could hear was laughter, horrible, awful, evil, laughter.

I woke up the next morning in a cold sweat. After taking a few deep breaths I looked over and saw that a few of James' action figures were positioned facing me on top of my nightstand. I sighed, James had probably woken up early and put these here. I gathered up the toys and made my way to James' room, however when I opened the door James was sound asleep. I just shrugged and placed the toys back into his toy box, and headed out to the living room. A little while later James woke up and I made him his breakfast. He was quiet and seemed a bit groggy, perhaps he didn't sleep well either. I decided to ask him about the toys, "James honey, did you put the toys in mommy's room this morning?" His eyes shot up at me for a moment then quickly glanced back down at his cereal. "Laughing Jack did it." I rolled my eyes and responded, "Well you tell 'Laughing Jack' to keep the toys in your room." James nodded and finished up his breakfast, then decided to go play out in the back yard.

I went to relax in the living room and I must have dozed off, because I woke up a couple hours later. "Shit! I need to check on James." I was a bit worried, it had been over 2 hours and I haven't checked on him. I went stepped out into the backyard, but James wasn't there anymore. I was getting nervous so I called out to him, "JAMES! JAMES WHERE ARE YOU?!" Just then I heard a giggle come from the front yard. I rushed through the gate around to the front of the house. James was sitting on the sidewalk. I breathed a sigh of relief and walked over to him, "James how many times have I told you to stay in the backya… James, what are you eating?" James looked up at me then reached into his pocket and pulled out a hand full of hard candies in all colors. This made me very nervous, "James, who gave you that candy?" James just stared at me not speaking. "JAMES! Please, tell mommy where you got that candy." James hung his head down and said "Laughing Jack gave it to me." My heart sunk, I kneeled down to look him in the eye, "James I've had had enough of this damn Laughing Jack thing, HE IS NOT REAL! Now this is a very serious situation and I need to know who gave you the candy!" I could see my son's eyes tear up, "But mama, Laughing Jack DID give me the candy." I closed my eyes and took a deep breath, James has never lied to me but what he's telling me is impossible. I make him spit out the candy and I throw the rest away, James appears to be fine. Maybe I'm just overreacting after all he could have gotten it from Tom and Linda from next door, or Mr. Walker down the street. Either way I'm going to have to keep a closer eye on James. That night I put James to bed as usual, and decided to go to bed early myself.

Suddenly I was woken up by a loud bang coming from the kitchen. I sprung out of bed and hurried down the stairs. When I got to the kitchen I was horrified. Everything on the counters had been thrown on the floor, and our dog Fido hung dead from the light fixture. His stomach was cut open and stuffed with candy, the same type that James was eating earlier that day. My shock was quickly broken by a sharp scream coming from James' room followed by loud crashes. I quickly grabbed a knife from the drawer and moved up the stairs with the speed that only a mother whose child is in danger could have. I burst through the door and flicked on the lights. Everything in the room was knocked over and tossed on the floor, my poor son in his bed crying and shaking with fear, a pool of urine staining the sheets. I scooped my child up and ran out of the house and went next door to Tom and Linda's house, luckily they were still awake. They let me use their phone and I called the police. It didn't take them long to arrive, and I explained what had happened, they looked at me as if I were crazy. They searched the house, but all they found was a dead dog and 2 trashed rooms. The officer told me that someone had probably gotten into the house and done this right before making a quick escape when they heard me coming up the stairs. I knew it wasn't true. All the doors were locked and none of the windows were open, whatever was in my house didn't come from outside.

The next day James stayed inside, I didn't want him to leave my sight. I went into the garage and found his old baby monitor and set it up in his room, if anything comes into his room tonight, I was going to be able to hear it. I went to the kitchen and grabbed the largest knife from the drawer and put it on my nightstand. Imaginary friend or not, I'm not letting anything hurt my little boy.

Soon enough night came. I put James to bed, he was afraid, but I promised him that I wasn't going to let anything happen to him. I tucked him in, gave him a kiss, and turned on the nightlight. Before closing the door I whispered to him "Goodnight James, I love you."

I tried to stay up as long as I could, but after a few hours I felt myself drifting off. My baby would be safe for the night and I needed to sleep. Just as I lay my head on the pillow I heard a soft noise come from the baby monitor I had put on my nightstand. At first it sounded like interference, like the kind a radio would make. Then it turned into a soft moan. Was James asleep? Then I heard it, the laugh from my nightmare, that horrible laugh. I sprung up from bed and grabbed the knife from under my pillow. I rushed over to James' room and creaked the door open. I tried the light switch but it wouldn't come on. I took a step in and I could feel the warm thick liquid on my feet. Suddenly James' nightlight came on and I could see the absolute horror laid out in front of me.

James' body was nailed up on the wall, the nails piercing through his hands and feet. His chest was cut wide open and his organs hung down to the floor. His eyes and tongue had been removed along with most of his teeth. I was disgusted, I could hardly believe this was my baby boy. Then I heard it again, the soft desperate moan. JAMES WAS STILL ALIVE! My baby, my poor baby, in so much pain barely clinging to life. I ran across the room and vomited on the floor, but my sickness was interrupted by a horrible cackle coming from behind me. I spun around while still wiping bile from my mouth, then out of the shadows emerged the fiend responsible for all this horror, Laughing Jack. His ghost white skin and matted black hair hung down to his shoulders. He had piercing white eyes surrounded by dark black rings. His twisted smile revealed a row of sharp jagged teeth, and his skin didn't look like skin at all, it almost looked like rubber or plastic. He wore a patchy, black and white clown outfit with striped sleeved and socks. His body itself was grotesque, his long arms hanging down past his waist and the way he was poised made him look almost boneless, like a ragdoll. He let out a sickening laugh as if to let me know he was pleased with my reaction to his 'work'. He then turned around slowly in front of James and began to laugh even more at the horrific sight he has laid out. That was enough to shake me from my terror, I snapped, "GET AWAY FROM HIM YOU BASTARD!" I rushed at the monster raising the knife above my head, and stabbed down at him, but as soon as the knife touched him he disappeared in a cloud of black smoke. The knife passed right through and pierced James' still beating heart, splashing the warm blood on my face….

No… what have I done? My baby, I killed my baby! I immediately fell to my knees, and I could hear sirens in the distance growing louder… My boy, my sweet baby boy… I promised mommy would protect you… But I failed… I'm sorry James… I'm so sorry…

Police soon arrived to find me in front of my son, still wielding the knife covered in my baby's blood. The trial was short, insanity. I was placed in the Phiropoulos House for the Criminally Insane, where I have been for the past 2 months. It's not so bad here, the only reason I'm awake now is because someone is playing Pop Goes the Weasel outside my window… I'll talk to the orderlies about it in the morning…

Smile dog

By unknown

I first met in person with Mary E. in the summer of 2007. I had arranged with her husband of fifteen years, Terence, to see her for an interview. Mary had initially agreed, since I was not a newsman but rather an amateur writer gathering information for a few early college assignments and, if all went according to plan, some pieces of fiction. We scheduled the interview for a particular weekend when I was in Chicago on unrelated business, but at the last moment Mary changed her mind and locked herself in the couple's bedroom, refusing to meet with me. For half an hour I sat with Terence as we camped outside the bedroom door, I listening and taking notes while he attempted fruitlessly to calm his wife.

The things Mary said made little sense but fit with the pattern I was expecting: though I could not see her, I could tell from her voice that she was crying, and more often than not her objections to speaking with me centered around an incoherent diatribe on her dreams — her nightmares. Terence apologized profusely when we ceased the exercise, and I did my best to take it in stride; recall that I wasn't a reporter in search of a story, but merely a curious young man in search of information. Besides, I thought at the time, I could perhaps find another, similar case if I put my mind and resources to it.

Mary E. was the sysop for a small Chicago-based Bulletin Board System in 1992 when she first encountered smile.jpg and her life changed forever. She and Terence had been married for only five months. Mary was one of an estimated 400 people who saw the image when it was posted as a hyperlink on the BBS, though she is the only one who has spoken openly about the experience. The rest have remained anonymous, or are perhaps dead.

In 2005, when I was only in tenth grade, smile.jpg was first brought to my attention by my burgeoning interest in web-based phenomena; Mary was the most often cited victim of what is sometimes referred to as "Smile.dog", the being smile.jpg is reputed to display. What caught my interest (other than the obvious macabre elements of the cyber-legend and my proclivity toward such things) was the sheer lack of information, usually to the point that people don't believe it even exists other than as a rumor or hoax.

It is unique because, though the entire phenomenon centers on a picture file, that file is nowhere to be found on the internet; certainly many photo manipulated simulacra litter the web, showing up with the most frequency on sites such as the image board 4chan, particularly the /x/-focused paranormal sub board. It is suspected these are fakes because they do not have the effect the true smile.jpg is believed to have, namely sudden onset temporal lobe epilepsy and acute anxiety.

This purported reaction in the viewer is one of the reasons the phantom-like smile.jpg is regarded with such disdain, since it is patently absurd, though depending on whom you ask the reluctance to acknowledge smile.jpg's existence might be just as much out of fear as it is out of disbelief.

Neither smile.jpg nor Smile.dog is mentioned anywhere on Wikipedia, though the website features articles on such other, perhaps more scandalous shock sites as ****** (hello.jpg) or 2girls1cup; any attempt to create a page pertaining to smile.jpg is summarily deleted by any of the encyclopedia's many admins.

Encounters with smile.jpg are the stuff of internet legend. Mary E.'s story is not unique; there are unverified rumors of smile.jpg showing up in the early days of Usenet and even one persistent tale that in 2002 a hacker flooded the forums of humor and satire website Something Awful with a deluge of Smile.dog pictures, rendering almost half the forum's users at the time epileptic.

It is also said that in the mid-to-late 90s that smile.jpg circulated on usenet and as an attachment of a chain email with the subject line "SMILE!! GOD LOVES YOU!" Yet despite the huge exposure these stunts would generate, there are very few people who admit to having experienced any of them and no trace of the file or any link has ever been discovered.

Those who claim to have seen smile.jpg often weakly joke that they were far too busy to save a copy of the picture to their hard drive. However, all alleged victims offer the same description of the photo: A dog-like creature (usually described as appearing similar to a Siberian husky), illuminated by the flash of the camera, sits in a dim room, the only background detail that is visible being a human hand extending from the darkness near the left side of the frame. The hand is empty, but is usually described as "beckoning". Of course, most attention is given to the dog (or dog-creature, as some victims are more certain than others about what they claim to have seen). The muzzle of the beast is reputedly split in a wide grin, revealing two rows of very white, very straight, very sharp, very human-looking teeth.

This is, of course, not a description given immediately after viewing the picture, but rather a recollection of the victims, who claim to have seen the picture endlessly repeated in their mind's eye during the time they are, in reality, having epileptic fits. These fits are reported to continue indeterminably, often while the victims sleep, resulting in very vivid and disturbing nightmares. These may be treated with medication, though in some cases it is more effective than others.

Mary E., I assumed, was not on effective medication. That was why after my visit to her apartment in 2007 I sent out feelers to several folklore- and urban legend-oriented newsgroups, websites, and mailing lists, hoping to find the name of a supposed victim of smile.jpg who felt more interested in talking about his experiences. For a time nothing happened and at length I forgot completely about my pursuits, since I had begun my freshman year of college and was quite busy. Mary contacted me via email, however, near the beginning of March 2008.

To: jml@****.com
From: marye@****.net
Subj: Last summer's interview

Dear Mr. L.,

I am incredibly sorry about my behavior last summer when you came to interview me. I hope you understand that it was no fault of yours, but rather my own problems that led me to act out as I did. I realized that I could have handled the situation more decorously; however, I hope you will forgive me. At the time, I was afraid.

You see, for fifteen years I have been haunted by smile.jpg. Smile.dog comes to me in my sleep every night. I know that sounds silly, but it is true. There is an ineffable quality about my dreams, my nightmares, that makes them completely unlike any real dreams I have ever had. I do not move and do not speak. I simply look ahead, and the only thing ahead of me is the scene from that horrible picture. I see the beckoning hand, and I see Smile.dog. It talks to me.

It is not a dog, of course, though I am not quite sure what it really is. It tells me it will leave me alone if only I do as it asks. All I must do, it says, is "spread the word". That is how it phrases its demands. And I know exactly what it means: it wants me to show it to someone else.

And I could. The week after my incident I received in the mail a manila envelope with no return address. Inside was only a 3 ½ -inch floppy diskette. Without having to check, I knew precisely what was on it.

I thought for a long time about my options. I could show it to a stranger, a coworker… I could even show it to Terence, as much as the idea disgusted me. And what would happen then? Well, if Smile.dog kept its word I could sleep. Yet if it lied, what would I do? And who was to say something worse would not come for me if I did as the creature asked?

So I did nothing for fifteen years, though I kept the diskette hidden amongst my things. Every night for fifteen years Smile.dog has come to me in my sleep and demanded that I spread the word. For fifteen years I have stood strong, though there have been hard times. Many of my fellow victims on the BBS board where I first encountered smile.jpg stopped posting; I heard some of them committed suicide. Others remained completely silent, simply disappearing off the face of the web. They are the ones I worry about the most.

I sincerely hope you will forgive me, Mr. L., but last summer when you contacted me and my husband about an interview I was near the breaking point. I decided I was going to give you the floppy diskette. I did not care if Smile.dog was lying or not, I wanted it to end. You were a stranger, someone I had no connection with, and I thought I would not feel sorrow when you took the diskette as part of your research and sealed your fate.

Before you arrived I realized what I was doing: was plotting to ruin your life. I could not stand the thought, and in fact I still cannot. I am ashamed, Mr. L., and I hope that this warning will dissuade you from further investigation of smile.jpg. You may in time encounter someone who is, if not weaker than I, then wholly more depraved, someone who will not hesitate to follow Smile.dog's orders.

Stop while you are still whole.

Sincerely,
Mary E.

Terence contacted me later that month with the news that his wife had killed herself. While cleaning up the various things she'd left behind, closing email accounts and the like, he happened upon the above message. He was a man in shambles; he wept as he told me to listen to his wife's advice. He'd found the diskette, he revealed, and burned it until it was nothing but a stinking pile of blackened plastic. The part that most disturbed him, however, was how the diskette had hissed as it melted. Like some sort of animal, he said.

I will admit that I was a little uncertain about how to respond to this. At first I thought perhaps it was a joke, with the couple belatedly playing with the situation in order to get a rise out of me. A quick check of several Chicago newspapers' online obituaries, however, proved that Mary E. was indeed dead. There was, of course, no mention of suicide in the article. I decided that, for a time at least, I would not further pursue the subject of smile.jpg, especially since I had finals coming up at the end of May.

But the world has odd ways of testing us. Almost a full year after I'd returned from my disastrous interview with Mary E., I received another email:

To: jml@****.com
From: elzahir82@****.com
Subj: smile

Hello

I found your e-mail address thru a mailing list your profile said you are interested in smiledog. I have saw it, it is not as bad as everyone says I have sent it to you here. Just spreading the word.

:)

The final line chilled me to the bone.

According to my email client there was one file attachment called, naturally, smile.jpg. I considered downloading it for some time. It was mostly likely a fake, I imagined, and even if it weren't I was never wholly convinced of smile.jpg's peculiar powers. Mary E.'s account had shaken me, yes, but she was probably mentally unbalanced anyway. After all, how could a simple image do what smile.jpg was said to accomplish? What sort of creature was it that could break one's mind with only the power of the eye?

And if such things were patently absurd, then why did the legend exist at all?

If I downloaded the image, if I looked at it, and if Mary turned out to be correct, if Smile.dog came to me in my dreams demanding I spread the word, what would I do? Would I live my life as Mary had, fighting against the urge to give in until I died? Or would I simply spread the word, eager to be put to rest? And if I chose the latter route, how could I do it? Whom would I burden in turn?

If I went through with my earlier intention to write a short article about smile.jpg, I decided, I could attach it as evidence. And anyone who read the article, anyone who took interest, would be affected. And even assuming the smile.jpg attached to the email was genuine, would I be capricious enough to save myself in that manner?

Could I spread the word?

Yes. Yes I could.

Robert the Doll

By Creepym0nsta

In the late 1800s, Thomas Otto and his family moved in to a mansion at the corner of Eaton and Simonton streets in Key West, Florida now known as the Artist House. The Otto's were known to be stern with their servants, sometimes even mistreating them. It was the treatment of one such Haitian servant that provides a twist in this story.

This woman was hired to take care of their son, Robert. One day, Mrs. Otto supposedly witnessed her practicing black magic in their backyard and fired her.

Before she left, the woman gave Robert a lifelike doll which stood 3 feet tall, had buttons for eyes, human hair (believed to be Robert's), and was filled with straw.

Dolls that resembled children were not unheard of during this time, but this one proved to be special. Robert named the doll after himself and often dressed it in his clothes. Robert, the doll, became his trustworthy companion. He took it with him on shopping trips into town. The doll had a seat at the dinner table where Robert would sneak it bites of food when his parents weren't looking. Robert would even be tucked into bed with the boy at night. Soon this innocent relationship took on a strange nature.

Soon after, Robert chose to be referred to by his middle name, Gene, after being scolded by his Mother. He told her that Robert was the doll's name, not his. Gene was often heard in his toy room having conversations with Robert. Gene would say something in his childish manner and responses could be heard in a much lower voice. Sometimes Gene would become very agitated, worrying the servants and his mother. She would, on occasion, burst in to find her son cowering in a corner while Robert sat perched in a chair or on the bed glaring at him. This was only the beginning.

Household objects would be found thrown across the room, Gene's toys turned up mutilated, and giggling could be heard. Whenever these unusual acts took place, Gene always said, "Robert did it!" The boy took the punishment but always insisted that the blame was Robert's. As the mischief grew, more and more servants took their leave as new ones were hired. The Otto's' relatives felt it was time to do something. With the recommendation of a great aunt, Gene's parents removed Robert from his care and placed him in a box in the attic. This is where he resided for many years.

After the death of his father, Gene was willed his boyhood home. He decided to live in the Victorian mansion with his new wife. Gene had become an artist, and felt the house was spacious and would provide a place for him to paint. He went to the attic and dusted off his childhood toy. He became attached to the doll despite his wife's displeasure. Gene would take the doll along with them everywhere they went. He even sat in his favorite little chair while Gene and his wife slept nearby. The Turret Room became Robert's domain after Mrs. Otto moved him back to the attic. Their marriage slowly became sour until Mrs. Otto supposedly went insane and died of unknown reasons. Gene followed soon behind.

Robert supposedly attacked people, sometimes locking them in the attic. People who passed by claimed to hear evil laughter coming from the Turret Room. For some time, Robert remained in the empty house by himself until a new family purchased the mansion and restored it. The doll was once again moved to the attic. This pleased it as much as the last time. The doll was often found throughout the house. On one certain night, Robert was found at the foot of the owners' bed giggling with a kitchen knife in hand. This was enough to send them fleeing from the home.

Robert was later moved to the East Martello Museum in Key West, where he sits perched in a glass box. Despite his new living quarters, the doll is believed to not have given up his menacing ways. Visitors and employees claim they have seen the doll move. His smile has been known to turn into a scowl. One employee cleaned Robert, turned off all the lights and left for the night.

The next day, he returned to find lights turned on, Robert sitting in a different position than the night before and a fresh layer of dust on his shoes. Some say he'll even curse you. If you want to take a picture of him, you must ask politely. He'll tilt his head in permission. However, if he doesn't and you take the picture anyways, a curse will befall upon you and anyone who accompanied you to the museum. The same will happen if you make fun of him.

To this day, Robert remains at the East Martello Museum in his sailor suit clutching his stuffed lion, continuing his menacing ways.

Sonic.exe

By unknown

I'm a total Sonic the Hedgehog fan much like everyone else, I like the newer games, but I don't mind playing the classics. I don't think I've ever played glitchy or hacked games before, though I don't think I want to play any after the experience I had...

It started on a nice summer afternoon, I was playing Sonic Unleashed (I liked how you get to explore the towns in it) until I noticed, out of my peripheral vision, that the mailman had arrived and put something in my mailbox as usual and left. I paused my game to go see what I got in the mail... The only thing in the Mailbox was a CD case for computers and a note. I took it inside.

I looked at the note first and realized it was from my dear friend Kyle (Let's just call him that), whom I hadn't heard from in 2 weeks. I know that because I recognized his handwriting, though what was weird is how it looked; it looked badly written and scratchy and somewhat difficult to read, as if Kyle was having a hard time writing it down and did it in a hurry.

This is what he wrote...

"Tom,

I can't take it anymore, I had to get rid of this thing somehow before it was too late, and I was hoping you'd do it for me. I can't do it, he's after me, and if you don't destroy this CD, he'll come after you too, he's too fast for me....

Please Tom, destroy this god-forsaken disc before he comes after you too, it's too late for me.
Destroy the disc, and you'll destroy him, but do it quick otherwise he'll catch you. Don't even play the game, it's what he wants, just destroy it.
Please...
Kyle"

Well, that was certainly weird. Even though Kyle IS my best friend and I haven't seen him in 2 weeks, I didn't do what he asked me. I didn't think that a simple gaming disc would do anything bad to him, after all it's just a game right? Boy, was I wrong about that...

ANY way, I looked at the disc and it looks like any ordinary computer CD-R disc, except it had black marker on it written "SONIC.EXE", and it was much unlike Kyle's handwriting, meaning that he must've gotten it from someone else, like a pawn shop or eBay. When I saw "SONIC" on the writing of the CD, I was actually excited and wanted to play it, since I'm a a BIG Sonic fan.

I went up to my room and turned on my computer and put the disc in and installed the game. When the title screen popped up I noticed that it was the first Sonic game, I was like "Awesome!" Because like I said earlier I liked the classics. The first thing I noticed that was out of place was when I pressed start, there's was a split second when I saw the title image turned into something much different, something that I now consider horrifying, before cutting to black.

I remember what the image looked like in that split second before the game cut to black; the sky had darkened, the title emblem was rusted and ruined, the SEGA 1991 was now instead SEGA 666, and the water had turned red, like blood, except it looked hyper-realistic.

But the freakiest thing that was in that split second frame was Sonic, his eyes were pitch black and bleeding with two glowing red dots staring RIGHT AT ME, and his smile had stretched wider up to the edge of his face. I was rather disturbed about that image when I saw it, though I figured that it was just a glitch and forgot about it. After it cut to black it stayed like that for about 10 seconds or so. And then another weird thing happened, the save file select from Sonic the Hedgehog 3 popped up, and I was like "WTF? What's this doing in the first Sonic game?", anyway, then I notice something off, the background was the dark cloudy sky of the Bad Stardust Speedway level from Sonic CD, and there were only three save files. The music was that creepy Caverns of Winter music from Earthbound, only it was extended and seemed to have been in reverse. And the image for the save file where you see a preview of the level you're on is just red static for all three files.

What freaked me out more was the character select, it showed only Tails, Knuckles and to my surprise, Dr. Robotnik! Now I was sure that something was up, I mean, how can you play as Robotnik in a classic Sonic game, for crying out loud?

That's when I realized that this wasn't a glitchy game, it was a hacked game.

Yeah it definitely looked hacked, it was really creepy, but as a smart gamer, I wasn't scared (or at least I tried not to be), I told myself that it was just a hacked game and there's nothing wrong with that. Anyways, shaking off the creeped out feeling I picked File 1 and chose Tails and when I selected and got started. The game froze for about 5 seconds and I heard a creepy pixelated laugh that sounded an awful lot like that Kefka guy from Final Fantasy before cutting to black.

The screen stayed black for about 10 seconds or more, then it showed the typical level title thing, except the simplistic shapes were different shades of red and the text showed only "HILL, ACT 1". The screen faded in and the level title vanished revealing Tails in the Green Hill Zone from Sonic 1, the music was different though, it sounded like a peaceful melody in reverse. Anyway I started playing and had Tails start running like you would in any of the classic Sonic games, what was odd was that as Tails was running along the level there was nothing but flat ground and a few trees for 5 minutes, that was when the peaceful music started to lower down into slow deep tones very slowly as I kept going.

I suddenly saw something and I stopped to see what it was; it was one of the small animals lying dead on the ground bleeding (That was when the music started to slow down), Tails had a shocked and saddened look on his face that I never saw him have before, so I had him move along, and he kept that worried look on his face. As he kept moving I saw more dead animals as Tails moved past them looking more and more worried as the music lowers and he moves past more dead animals, I was shocked to see how they all died, they looked like somebody killed them in rather gruesome ways; a squirrel was hanged on a tree with what appeared to be his entrails hanging out, a bunny had all four of his limbs torn off and a duck had his eyes gouged out and his throat slit. I felt sick to my stomach when I saw this massacre and apparently so did Tails. After a few more seconds there were no more animals and the music seemed to have stopped, I still kept Tails to continue. After a minute passed after the music stopped, Tails was running up a hill and then he stopped, it wasn't until I saw why; Sonic was there on the other side of the screen with his back against Tails with his eyes closed. Tails looked happy to see Sonic but then his smile faltered, obviously noticing that Sonic wasn't responding to him, if not acting as if he was totally oblivious of Tails' presence. Tails walked slowly toward Sonic, and I noticed that I wasn't even moving my keyboard to make him move, so this had to have been a cut scene.

Suddenly I began to have a growing feel of dread as Tails walked closer to Sonic to get his attention, I felt that Tails was in danger and something bad was going to happen. I heard faint static growing louder as Tails was but inches away from Sonic and stopped and stuck his hand out to touch him. That foreboding feeling in my gut was growing stronger and I felt the urge to tell Tails to get away from Sonic as the static grew louder.

Suddenly in a split second I saw Sonic's eyes open and they were black with those red glowing dots, just like that title image, thought there wasn't a smile. When that happened the screen turned black and the static sound was off.

It stayed black for about 7 seconds and then white text appeared forming a message, saying, "Hello. Do you want to play with me?"

At this point I was creeped out, I didn't want to continue

with the game, but my curiosity got the better of me when I was taken to a different level with the level title now saying "HIDE AND SEEK".

This time I was in the Angel Island level from Sonic 3 and it looked like everything was on fire.

Tails looked as though he was scared out of his wits this time. He actually looked at me and made frantic gestures to me as if he wanted to get out of the area he was in as fast as possible. I was starting to get freaked out by this...I mean Tails was actually breaking the fourth wall, trying to tell me to get him out of there.

So I pressed down on the arrow key as hard as I could and made him run as fast as he could, a pixelated version of that creepy theme when you meet Shadow at the ARK as Robotnik from SA2 was playing as I made Tails trek through the desolate forest, trying to help him escape from whatever he was trying to run from.

Suddenly I heard that creepy laugh again... that awful, Kefka laugh... right after 10 seconds have passed as I helped Tails run through the forest, and then I started seeing flashes of Sonic popping everywhere on the screen, again with those black and red eyes.

The music changed to that suspenseful drowning jingle as I see Sonic behind Tails slowly gaining up on him FLYING; Sonic wasn't running, he was actually FLYING! The flying pose his sprite was making looked very similar to Metal Sonic's flying pose in Sonic CD, except it was just Sonic and he had the black and red eyes again, only

THIS time he had the most deranged looking grin on his face, he looked as though he was enjoying the torment he was giving the poor little fox as he gained up on him.

Suddenly when Tails tripped (another cut scene) the music stopped and Sonic vanished. Tails laid there and started crying for 15 seconds. The scene was rather upsetting to watch and I kind of teared up myself. But then Sonic appeared right in front of Tails and Tails looked up in horror.

Blood started to come down those blackened eyes of Sonic's as a grin slowly grew from his face as he looked down at the horrified fox, I could do nothing but watch. Just in a split second Sonic lunged at Tails right before the screen went black, there was a loud screeching noise that only lasted 5 seconds. The text returned only this time it said "You're too slow, want to try again?" and then that god-awful laugh came with it.

I was so shocked by what had happened...did Sonic murder Tails? No, he couldn't have... He and Tails are supposed to be best friends, right? Why did Sonic do that to him?

I shook the shock off as I was brought back to the character select, the save file that had Tails was different; Tails was no longer in the box itself but in the TV screen itself, which was flickering with that red static, Tails' expression scared me, his eyes were black and bleeding, his orange fur had gone black and he had an expression of anguish on his face, Trying to ignore it I picked Knuckles next.

The laugh came again and the screen cut to black again and stayed there for another 10 seconds, this time the level said "YOU CAN'T RUN".

I was really freaked out by now, I couldn't really tell if this was a glitch, or a hack, or some kind of sick twisted joke... or anything really. But despite my fear of what happened next, I kept playing.

The next level looked much different, it had the ground of the Scrap Brain zone, but the sky background looked like the main menu; it had the dark reddish cloudy sky. But it was the music that creeped me out the most: It sounded like Giygas' theme right after you beat Pokey in Earthbound. I also noticed that Knuckles looked afraid just like Tails did, though not as much, more rather he looked a little unnerved. He broke the fourth wall just like Tails and looked as if he wasn't sure about going on, but I made him move anyway.

He ran down the straight pathway in this dark level, and as he did the screen started to flicker red static a couple times and then that maddening laugh came again.

Then after a few seconds of running I notice several bloodstains on the metallic ground, I felt a growing sense of fear again thinking something horrible is going to happen to Knuckles. He looked nauseated walking down this blood-stained road, but I still kept him going.

Suddenly as Knuckles ran, Sonic appeared right in front of him with those black and red eyes and then red static appeared again, when the static vanished showing nothing but black screen with text saying "FOuNd YOu!", I was now scared, Sonic found Knuckles already?! What was going on?!

Anyway red static came again and then I was back to the level, Knuckles looked like he was panicking, and Sonic was nowhere to be found. And this time that high-pitched squealing from the Silent Hill 1's final boss was playing. Was this some kind of boss battle with Sonic? I hoped to God it wasn't, honestly.

Suddenly Sonic appeared right behind Knuckles in what appeared to be pixelated black smoke, I made Knuckles turn and then punch Sonic, but Sonic vanished in black pixelated smoke before I could even land a hit, that terrible laugh went off again. Then Sonic appeared behind Knuckles again and then I made him punch again, and Sonic vanished again laughing. Knuckles was panicking even more, and even I felt like I was going crazy, Sonic was practically playing with us, he was playing a sick twisted little mind game with me and Knuckles...

Another cut scene played as Knuckled fell to his knees and clutched his head sobbing, I felt his agony, Sonic was actually driving us BOTH crazy.

And then in a split second Sonic lunged at Knuckles and the screen went black with another distorted screeching noise that lasted for at least 3 seconds.

Another text message appeared, "So many souls to play with, so little time... would you agree?"

What the hell... Just what is going on? I started to think Sonic was actually trying to talk to me through the game... But I was too scared to think that.

I was brought back to the main menu and this time the second file box had Knuckles in the TV screen, his red fur had darkened to a reddish grey, his dreadlocks were dripping with blood and his eyes were black and bleeding too, and he had a look of sadness on his face. I began to think that those are the actual characters trapped in those TV screens on the save files, but I couldn't believe it... I didn't want to believe it...

So I shut off the game and took a break. I took a nap, wish I hadn't, 'cause I then began to have the most disturbing nightmare, I was in pitch black darkness, though I was under the light given off by a lamp that hung high above my head. I could hear the cries of Knuckles and Tails nearby. They were saying stuff like, "Help us..." and "Why did you give us to him?" and "Run away, before he gets you too..."

Their cries died out as I then heard Sonic laugh, his laugh... it sounded a lot like the distorted Kefka laugh.

"You're a lot fun to play with kid, just like your friend Kyle, though he didn't last long..."

I was scared and looking around for the source of the voice...

"Won't be long now until you join him and all my other friends..."

I saw him walking toward me, flickering in and out in several directions...

"You can't run, kid. You're in my world now. Just like the others..."

When he grabbed me and I saw his bleeding black and red-eyed, grinning face, I woke up with a fright.

After a couple of hours I decided to continue playing the game. I don't know why, but I had to know, I had to figure out why this was happening... So I turned on the computer, turned on the game and selected Robotnik next.

I still thought that was wacky, playing as Robotnik, but anyway the level title appeared again and this time it said "...", which I found really freaky.

This time I was in some kind of hallway, didn't really look like it was from any of the classic Sonic games, though it has the pixelated style; the floor was shiny and checkered, the walls were a dark greyish purple with animated candlelight's and a few dark bloodstains here and there, and there was a dark red curtain hanging above on the top part of the screen. Every 12 seconds or so that red curtain sways very slowly, but whenever you're playing the game you can barely see it move. The music was oddly pleasant, a piano playing a rather sad yet peaceful song, but I knew better, this was the song that played in Hill act 1, only it wasn't in reverse.

Robotnik didn't look entirely nervous like Tails and Knuckles did, but he did have a suspicious look on his face as if he was just a bit paranoid. He did a little animation when I just left him standing, he turns his head to the left and then to the right at least twice and then shrugs at me, as if he has no idea where he was or what was going on. Even though I was scared outta my mind about what was going to happen, I had Robotnik continue onward. He did his usual running animation (You know, when you've beaten him at the end of a classic Sonic game and you chase him) as we continued going through the hallway. Then I stop at a long flight of stairs leading downward, now I was nervous, even Robotnik seemed unsure of himself, though I pressed onward.

As I led Robotnik down the stairs, I noticed that the walls have gotten darker and more reddish; the red torches are now an eerie blue. Then we landed onto another hallway, this one was longer than the last one (or at least it felt like it) and then we headed down another flight of stairs down, this one was much longer, took at least 1 full minute. And then I heard that horrid Kefka laugh again and then the music slowly faded until it was quiet, as it did the walls turned more dark red and the torches were a black flame now.

When Robotnik landed onto the 3rd hallway, I noticed he now looked really creeped out, though he tried to hide it, I couldn't blame him, I was scared too.

Suddenly, Sonic popped right in front of Robotnik the same way he did Knuckles and then red static. The red static lasted for about 15 second and then it showed me a most unpleasant image...

The image showed a hyper-realistic of Sonic standing in the darkness where you can only see his face while his head and torso faded into black, and when I say hyper-realistic, I mean like he looked so real you could actually see the lines in his blue fur, as if you could actually feel the fur if you touched the screen.

His face...oh god, he had the most horrifying smile I had ever seen.

And that's saying something considering I saw that image at the start of the game.

His eyes are wide and black and once again crying blood (Which also looked hyper-realistic) and there were two small glowing red dots in those black eyes staring RIGHT AT ME, as if staring into my mind. His grin was wide and demonic, it literally stretched to the sides of his face like a Cheshire Cat except Sonic had fangs, VERY SHARP fangs, much like the Werehog's teeth except more vicious-looking, somewhat yellowish and from the look of it, he had stains of blood and small bits of flesh on his lips and fangs as if he ate some animal.

I stared at that gruesome image for a good 30 seconds, never taking my eyes off it, I felt as if he was actually looking at me, smiling at me...that face, it just took 10 seconds for it to etch itself into my brain for good.

Then the screen flickered with red static again 3 times, and on the 3rd time I heard the Kefka laugh, except this time it sounded distorted, demonic even...

It went back to the image again except this time there was the text again though it was messed up, but it was pretty much one of the most horrifying things I looked at since I had this game...

"I AM GOD."

It was when I read that message while looking at Sonic when it hit me, I realized right there and then.

This Sonic was a monster, a pure evil, sadistic, all-powerful, nightmarish, demented monster... and all of his victims, including Tails, Knuckles, Robotnik and possibly Kyle, are just his little toys, and the game is the very gateway into his chaotic, nightmarish world and the very Hell his victims are trapped in.

Suddenly in an actual split second I screamed as Sonic lunged at the screen screeching loudly with his mouth wide open to an unnatural length revealing nothing but a literally spiraling abyss of pure darkness before the red static came again, this time much louder and distorted, so loud that it hurt my ears, I yelled and grabbed my ears as the red static screeched for a good 7 seconds.

Then it stopped and showed nothing but black screen.

As I sat there staring at the black screen, one last text came up.

"Ready for Round 2, Tom?"

The Kefka laugh, now sounding more clear as if Sonic was right behind me, played again 3 times as I looked at that text in shock and confusion.

Then I got booted back to the main menu and this time the third save file had a TV image of Robotnik in the same, tormented state as Tails and Knuckles; Robotnik's skin turned a dull grey, his mustache drooped and had blackened, his glasses broke and blood is coming from them and he had a mere dead like expression on his face.
I looked at Tails, Knuckles and Robotnik and I cried a bit, I pitied them for the agony they're going through, they were forever trapped within the game, forever tormented by that horrid hedgehog, and always will be.
Then the computer shut itself off, I couldn't turn it back on no matter what I did.
I sat there for maybe 25 seconds, horrified by what had just happened...
Sonic is the very embodiment of evil, he tortures people who play his game in more ways than one and then when he gets bored he drags you into the game, literally drags you to Hell, where he can play with you always, as his toy....
I can't get the game outta my computer. I think it's stuck in there, but at least I managed to turn it back on now.
After I sat there for 25 seconds I heard a voice right behind me, like a whisper...
"Try to keep this interesting for me, Tom."
I turned around to see where the voice came from, and what I saw made me scream...
Sitting on my bed... staring right at me...
... Was a Sonic plushie, smiling with bloodstains under its eyes.

The Midnight Man

By Archivistoflostsouls

I don't know where to start. Where to begin about my feelings of this "thing". This story is one that I have had to keep secret in fear that friends or family may persecute me and send me to a mental facility. What I have seen, what I have heard has been shot down by many as simple lies. This story hopefully will open the eyes to some who don't believe in my words of "it" and what it is.

Let me start off on a new note. The first time I encountered "it" was the late summer of 2008. My family's house had been foreclosed since we could just not afford to pay it off anymore because of all the land that we owned. We bought a smaller house in a nice neighborhood that was just about 2 miles away from the one prior. I guessed we just liked the area. It was all well for a while. I settled into the new home quite alright. It felt like home. It felt nice and pleasant, even when it rained. You felt safe, secure.

Then one day, after we were settled in, I decided to go for a walk on the nearby trail. No one else was there, not even as I looked as far in front of me and as I turned around, not even a single person. It seemed a bit odd. It was a nice day out. So why am I the only to enjoy the day on this sidewalk? Whatever, I guess that I shouldn't be complaining about having a trail to my lonesome self. I continued my trek and peered to both sides of the trail. To my left; a rather small but steep hill that led to more houses and to my right was just a thin woods teeming with green trees and dirt.

This woods ran across the trail the entire way. Being my boy-self, I jumped into this nest of foliage hoping to find some adventure. I looked around and examined everything I saw. I picked up a stick and began to swing it like sword. I continued inside the small, narrow woods to find something that mildly disturbed me. A small rabbit about the size of a large man's shoe laid dead across the leafy earthy floor. I dropped the stick and knelt down on one knee to examine it further.

Its stomach had been torn down the middle with the entrails barely seeping out. Something odder was that there seemed to be no bite marks, or scratches, as if it just seemed to...die. Then a weird feeling in the back of my head entered, a tingling feeling. It didn't hurt. But it was very irritating. It made me want to just hit my head against a tree to make it stop, but even as a child I knew that was foolish.

I didn't feel any more "adventure" in me after the rabbit so I trekked back home and ate supper without informing my family of the rabbit. The next morning I woke up to hear talking downstairs. My mom and my sister were talking about something on the deck. I woke up and looked to my mom who had a disgusted look on her face.

"What's going on?" I asked in a worried tone.

"I think an animal left some of its lunch on our porch." I looked out to see under our porch swing was a pile of animal entrails.

I whispered to myself "The rabbit.." My mom cleaned them off then threw them away. Nothing more happened during the day. It went on as all days go on. But that night I had a dream...or at least I thought that it was a dream.

It started out with me, in the woods. I was laying down in the same spot where I found the rabbit. I was cold. I was naked and I didn't have a clue what was happening. I couldn't move but I saw in the distance a shadowy figure that seemed to be constructed of the darkness. It seemed to almost be a good seven feet tall. He had a deer like shape for a head. Horns curled from his shoulders and back. He walked like a man by had hooves or what seemed to be hooves...I don't know!

He walked towards me, creeping past the trees. A once dark forest had been made even darker as a cloud of misty fog followed its trail. It spoke in a demonic, monotone voice. *"You think that you are of a higher importance then a rabbit? That you are greater?"* I couldn't respond; I was shocked at everything that was happening. He spoke once more. *"The earth will die and all will cry. Bring the tears of the unfaithful. The untrustworthy and the cynical men and women to me.*

They won't know me by an image but by their undying fate. Maybe they should of listened to the crazy man on the street, maybe they should've listened to the one who tried to convince them that it was no myth or of what they all saw was indeed, true flesh and fact. You know my son, that little 'thing' that just catches your curious eye. That little unnatural feeling that makes you feel out of place, that something's wrong. That physical feeling when you feel something touch you but you debunk it as just your mind? That is me. The Midnight Man."

He knelt to my level and with a soft yet noticeable touch he prodded my stomach with a pointed, sharp claw. He arose and walked away. I peered at my naked body. My stomach turned into a shadowy black and it traveled through my bare body. Just then I awakened in my bed sweating through my sheets. I glanced down to my pillow to see it covered in blood. I touched my face to feel blood dripping from my nose.

Since the day these events occurred, I have been seeing more and more things and my self being has changed. My grades in school dropped and I began to slack off and focus on the world out of school. The woods, my house...the "Midnight Man". Though I haven't seen or heard of him since, I can feel his presence within me. I don't know if he is evil or good. I do know that I know more about life and my self being after my encounter with him.

I still suffer from the tingling in my head and I always think about what he's said since that day. I believe that this man can enter anyone's thoughts and wellbeing and break you down until you change entirely. This thing is dangerous to anyone and whatever it, he, this thing is. It must be stopped....

Mr. Widemouth

By perfectcircle35

During my childhood my family was like a drop of water in a vast river, never remaining in one location for long. We settled in Rhode Island when I was eight, and there we remained until I went to college in Colorado Springs. Most of my memories are rooted in Rhode Island, but there are fragments in the attic of my brain which belong to the various homes we had lived in when I was much younger.

Most of these memories are unclear and pointless – chasing after another boy in the back yard of a house in North Carolina, trying to build a raft to float on the creek behind the apartment we rented in Pennsylvania, and so on. But there is one set of memories which remains as clear as glass, as though they were just made yesterday. I often wonder whether these memories are simply lucid dreams produced by the long sickness I experienced that spring, but in my heart, I know they are real.

We were living in a house just outside the bustling metropolis of New Vineyard, Maine, population 643. It was a large structure, especially for a family of three. There were a number of rooms that I didn't see in the five months we resided there. In some ways it was a waste of space, but it was the only house on the market at the time, at least within an hour's commute to my father's place of work.

The day after my fifth birthday (attended by my parents alone), I came down with a fever. The doctor said I had mononucleosis, which meant no rough play and more fever for at least another three weeks. It was horrible timing to be bed-ridden– we were in the process of packing our things to move to Pennsylvania, and most of my things were already packed away in boxes, leaving my room barren. My mother brought me ginger ale and books several times a day, and these served the function of being my primary form of entertainment for the next few weeks. Boredom always loomed just around the corner, waiting to rear its ugly head and compound my misery.

I don't exactly recall how I met Mr. Widemouth. I think it was about a week after I was diagnosed with mono. My first memory of the small creature was asking him if he had a name. He told me to call him Mr. Widemouth, because his mouth was large. In fact, everything about him was large in comparison to his body– his head, his eyes, his crooked ears– but his mouth was by far the largest.

"You look kind of like a Furby," I said as he flipped through one of my books.

Mr. Widemouth stopped and gave me a puzzled look. "Furby? What's a Furby?" he asked.

I shrugged. "You know… the toy. The little robot with the big ears. You can pet and feed them, almost like a real pet."

"Oh." Mr. Widemouth resumed his activity. "You don't need one of those. They aren't the same as having a real friend."

I remember Mr. Widemouth disappearing every time my mother stopped by to check in on me. "I lay under your bed," he later explained. "I don't want your parents to see me because I'm afraid they won't let us play anymore."

We didn't do much during those first few days. Mr. Widemouth just looked at my books, fascinated by the stories and pictures they contained. The third or fourth morning after I met him, he greeted me with a large smile on his face. "I have a new game we can play," he said. "We have to wait until after your mother comes to check on you, because she can't see us play it. It's a secret game."

After my mother delivered more books and soda at the usual time, Mr. Widemouth slipped out from under the bed and tugged my hand. "We have to go the room at the end of this hallway," he said. I objected at first, as my parents had forbidden me to leave my bed without their permission, but Mr. Widemouth persisted until I gave in.

The room in question had no furniture or wallpaper. Its only distinguishing feature was a window opposite the doorway. Mr. Widemouth darted across the room and gave the window a firm push, flinging it open. He then beckoned me to look out at the ground below.

We were on the second story of the house, but it was on a hill, and from this angle the drop was farther than two stories due to the incline. "I like to play pretend up here," Mr. Widemouth explained. "I pretend that there is a big, soft trampoline below this window, and I jump. If you pretend hard enough you bounce back up like a feather. I want you to try."

I was a five-year-old with a fever, so only a hint of skepticism darted through my thoughts as I looked down and considered the possibility. "It's a long drop," I said.

"But that's all a part of the fun. It wouldn't be fun if it was only a short drop. If it were that way you may as well just bounce on a real trampoline."

I toyed with the idea, picturing myself falling through thin air only to bounce back to the window on something unseen by human eyes. But the realist in me prevailed. "Maybe some other time," I said. "I don't know if I have enough imagination. I could get hurt."

Mr. Widemouth's face contorted into a snarl, but only for a moment. Anger gave way to disappointment. "If you say so," he said. He spent the rest of the day under my bed, quiet as a mouse.

The following morning Mr. Widemouth arrived holding a small box. "I want to teach you how to juggle," he said. "Here are some things you can use to practice, before I start giving you lessons."

I looked in the box. It was full of knives. "My parents will kill me!" I shouted, horrified that Mr. Widemouth had brought knives into my room– objects that my parents would never allow me to touch. "I'll be spanked and grounded for a year!"

Mr. Widemouth frowned. "It's fun to juggle with these. I want you to try it."

I pushed the box away. "I can't. I'll get in trouble. Knives aren't safe to just throw in the air."

Mr. Widemouth's frown deepened into a scowl. He took the box of knives and slid under my bed, remaining there the rest of the day. I began to wonder how often he was under me.

I started having trouble sleeping after that. Mr. Widemouth often woke me up at night, saying he put a real trampoline under the window, a big one, one that I couldn't see in the dark. I always declined and tried to go back to sleep, but Mr. Widemouth persisted. Sometimes he stayed by my side until early in the morning, encouraging me to jump.

He wasn't so fun to play with anymore.

My mother came to me one morning and told me I had her permission to walk around outside. She thought the fresh air would be good for me, especially after being confined to my room for so long. Ecstatic, I put on my sneakers and trotted out to the back porch, yearning for the feeling of sun on my face.

Mr. Widemouth was waiting for me. "I have something I want you to see," he said. I must have given him a weird look, because he then said, "It's safe, I promise."

I followed him to the beginning of a deer trail which ran through the woods behind the house. "This is an important path," he explained. "I've had a lot of friends about your age. When they were ready, I took them down this path, to a special place. You aren't ready yet, but one day, I hope to take you there."

I returned to the house, wondering what kind of place lay beyond that trail.

Two weeks after I met Mr. Widemouth, the last load of our things had been packed into a moving truck. I would be in the cab of that truck, sitting next to my father for the long drive to Pennsylvania. I considered telling Mr. Widemouth that I would be leaving, but even at five years old, I was beginning to suspect that perhaps the creature's intentions were not to my benefit, despite what he said otherwise. For this reason, I decided to keep my departure a secret.

My father and I were in the truck at 4 a.m. He was hoping to make it to Pennsylvania by lunch time tomorrow with the help of an endless supply of coffee and a six-pack of energy drinks. He seemed more like a man who was about to run a marathon rather than one who was about to spend two days sitting still.

"Early enough for you," my father asked with a hint of sympathy?

I nodded and placed my head against the window, hoping for some sleep before the sun came up. I felt my father's hand on my shoulder. "This is the last move, son, I promise. I know it's hard for you, as sick as you've been.

Once daddy gets promoted we can settle down and you can make friends."

I opened my eyes as we backed out of the driveway. I saw Mr. Widemouth's silhouette in my bedroom window. He stood motionless until the truck was about to turn onto the main road. He gave a pitiful little wave good-bye, steak knife in hand. I didn't wave back.

Years later, I returned to New Vineyard. The piece of land our house stood upon was empty except for the foundation, as the house burned down a few years after my family left. Out of curiosity, I followed the deer trail that Mr. Widemouth had shown me. Part of me expected him to jump out from behind a tree and scare the living bejeesus out of me, but I felt that Mr. Widemouth was gone, somehow tied to the house that no longer existed.

The trail ended at the New Vineyard Memorial Cemetery.

I noticed that many of the tombstones belonged to children.

Gateway of the Mind

By unknown

In 1983, a team of deeply pious scientists conducted a radical experiment in an undisclosed facility. The scientists had theorized that a human without access to any senses or ways to perceive stimuli would be able to perceive the presence of God.

They believed that the five senses clouded our awareness of eternity, and without them, a human could actually establish contact with God by thought. An elderly man who claimed to have "nothing left to live for" was the only test subject to volunteer. To purge him of all his senses, the scientists performed a complex operation in which every sensory nerve connection to the brain was surgically severed.* although the test subject retained full muscular function, he could not see, hear, taste, smell, or feel. With no possible way to communicate with or even sense the outside world, he was alone with his thoughts.

Scientists monitored him as he spoke aloud about his state of mind in jumbled, slurred sentences that he couldn't even hear. After four days, the man claimed to be hearing hushed, unintelligible voices in his head. Assuming it was an onset of psychosis, the scientists paid little attention to the man's concerns.

Two days later, the man cried that he could hear his dead wife speaking with him, and even more, he could communicate back. The scientists were intrigued, but were not convinced until the subject started naming dead relatives of the scientists. He repeated personal information to the scientists that only their dead spouses and parents would have known. At this point, a sizable portion of scientists left the study.

After a week of conversing with the deceased through his thoughts, the subject became distressed, saying the voices were overwhelming. In every waking moment, his consciousness was bombarded by hundreds of voices that refused to leave him alone. He frequently threw himself against the wall, trying to elicit a pain response. He begged the scientists for sedatives, so he could escape the voices by sleeping. This tactic worked for three days, until he started having severe night terrors. The subject repeatedly said that he could see and hear the deceased in his dreams.

Only a day later, the subject began to scream and claw at his non-functional eyes, hoping to sense something in the physical world. The hysterical subject now said the voices of the dead were deafening and hostile, speaking of hell and the end of the world. At one point, he yelled "No heaven, no forgiveness" for five hours straight. He continually begged to be killed, but the scientists were convinced that he was close to establishing contact with God.

After another day, the subject could no longer form coherent sentences. Seemingly mad, he started to bite off chunks of flesh from his arm. The scientists rushed into the test chamber and restrained him to a table so he could not kill himself. After a few hours of being tied down, the subject halted his struggling and screaming. He stared blankly at the ceiling as teardrops silently streaked across his face. For two weeks, the subject had to be manually rehydrated due to the constant crying. Eventually, he turned his head and, despite his blindness, made focused eye contact with a scientist for the first time in the study.

He whispered "I have spoken with God, and He has abandoned us" and his vital signs stopped.

There was no apparent cause of death.

follow-up study, 2000: Dr. G.F., Department of Neurology, [hospital name withheld], San Francisco, CA. Recent study of a degenerative disease which targets the motor function and cognitive decline often leads to 'hallucinations' of the deceased. The death of targeted cells and chemicals in the brain by this disease leads to a loss of smell, among other senses. The cause of the disease is unknown. Hallucinations present in 39.8% of the patients, falling into three categories: a sensation of a presence (person), a sideways passage (commonly of an animal) or illusions. Present in 25.5% of patients (an isolated occurrence in 14.3%), formed visual hallucinations present in 22.2% (isolated in 9.3%) and auditory hallucinations present in 9.7% (isolated in 2.3%). Continuing study in San Francisco, CA. 2003-present

The Expressionless

By Ivysir

In June 1972, a woman appeared in Cedar Senai hospital in nothing but a white, blood-covered gown.

Now this, in itself, should not be too surprising as people often have accidents nearby and come to the nearest hospital for medical attention, but there were two things that caused people who saw her to vomit and flee in terror.

The first being that she wasn't exactly human. She resembled something close to a mannequin, but had the dexterity and fluidity of a normal human being. Her face was as flawless as a mannequins, devoid of eyebrows and smeared in make-up.

There was a kitten clamped in her jaws so unnaturally tight that no teeth could be seen, and the blood was still squirting out over her gown and onto the floor. She then pulled it out of her mouth, tossed it aside and collapsed.

From the moment she stepped through the entrance to when she was taken to a hospital room and cleaned up before being prepped for sedation, she was completely calm, expressionless and motionless. The doctors thought it best to restrain her until the authorities could arrive and she did not protest. They were unable to get any kind of response from her and most staff members felt too uncomfortable to look directly at her for more than a few seconds.

But the second the staff tried to sedate her, she fought back with extreme force. Two members of staff had to hold her down as her body rose up on the bed with that same, blank expression.

She turned her emotionless eyes towards the male doctor and did something unusual. She smiled.

As she did, the female doctor screamed and let go out of shock. In the woman's mouth were not human teeth, but long, sharp spikes. Too long for her mouth to close fully without causing any damage…

The male doctor stared back at her for a moment before asking "What in the hell are you?"

She cracked her neck down to her shoulder to observe him, still smiling.

There was a long pause, the security had been alerted and could be heard coming down the hallway.

As he heard them approach, she darted forward, sinking her teeth into the front of his throat, ripping out his jugular and letting him fall to the floor, gasping for air as he choked on his own blood.

She stood up and leaned over him, her face coming dangerously close to his as the life faded from his eyes.

She leaned closer and whispered in his ear.

"I... am... God..."

The doctor's eyes filled with fear as he watched her calmly walk away to greet the security men. His last ever sight would be watching her feast on them one by one.

The female doctor who survived the incident named her "The Expressionless".

There was never a sighting of her again.

Doors

By unknown

I was adopted. I never knew my real mother; rather, I knew her at one time but I left her side when I was too little to be able to remember. I loved my adopted family though. They were so kind to me. I ate well, I lived in a warm and comfortable house, and I got to stay up pretty late.

Let me tell you about my family real fast: First, there's my mother. I never called her Mom or anything like that; I just called her by her first name. Janice. She didn't mind at all though. I called her that for so long, I don't think she even noticed. Anyhow, she was a very kind woman. I think that she is the one who recommended my adoption in the first place. Sometimes I would lay my head against her in front of the television and she would tickle my back with her nails. She is one of those Hollywood mothers.

Second, there's Dad. His real name was Richard, but he never really liked me much so I began to refer to him as Dad in a desperate attempt to gain his affection. It didn't work. I think that no matter what I called him, he would never love me as much as his own child. That's understandable so I really didn't press the matter. The most notable attribute of Dad was his unmoving sternness. He was not afraid to pop his children when they did something wrong. I found that out before I could use the restroom properly. He didn't hesitate to spank me. Well, I'm in line and it's because of his methods.

Lastly, is my sister. Little Emily was really young when I was adopted, so we were about the same age, but she was slightly older. I liked to think of her as my little sister, though. We got along better than any sibling could possibly get along. We would always stay up late together and just talk. Well, she did a lot of the talking; I mostly just listened because I loved her. It was a great setup that we had! We were short on bedrooms, so- because I didn't want to sleep in the living room by myself when I was littler- I had a pallet set up for me next to her bed on the floor. This is where I have slept since. But it was cool with me because I enjoyed being with her and I had always felt pretty protective of my little sis.

Everything changed on a horrible Wednesday night. I was at home taking a nap when little Emily opened the front door. The sound of the door opening pulled me to a state of consciousness and I walked from the room down the hall to the living room. That's when I first remembered it was Wednesday. I was never any good at keeping track of what day it was. Actually I'll just go ahead and say it: My sense of time was HORRIBLE! But nevertheless, I knew it was Wednesday because Emily had just come home from her Church's youth group gathering. She walked in the front door and hugged me, and then was followed in by Dad and Janice.

"You have a good nap?" Janice said teasingly as she ruffled up my hair. I just shook my head away and snorted in a manner that clearly expressed that I was teasing back with her.

"Don't you snort at your mother like that!" said my father gruffly with authority. He shut the door behind him and hung up his coat.

"I was clearly joking…" I growled under my breath. He must not have heard me because I didn't feel him smack me. Emily then proceeded to our room and I followed. She started telling me about her day. You know… usual teenage girl stuff. But I listened so that she would feel better. After her summary she suggested watching TV and I obliged and jumped onto the couch as she was going for the remote. She rolled her eyes at my little-brother-like immaturity and scooted me over and sat down. The TV turned on and we watched it together until the sun went down. Emily was the kind of girl that- instead of watching cartoons and soap operas- would rather watch Discovery and Animal Planet and Natural Geographic. I like those too so I didn't mind. Actually, those were the only channels that can hold my attention.

So it got late and Janice walked up behind the sofa. "Emily it's past your bed time. Turn off the television and go to your room. You too." she pointed at me. Emily turned off the program we were watching grudgingly and stood up. She started down the hallway to our room. As I followed I couldn't shake the feeling that something wasn't right.

We went into our room and Emily turned off the light. Just as she did, I caught a flash of movement out of the corner of my eye. It was out the window, but as soon as I redirected my line of sight to where the window was no longer in my peripheral vision, what it was that I thought I saw was gone. I still remained alert. For my sister's sake.

I laid there in the darkness with nothing but the thin ray of light from the street lamp outside to illuminate the room. It wasn't much. Time and time again I could have sworn that I heard subtle sounds just out the window… a twig break, leaves crunching, clothes jostling, and all the while I could smell a faint stench of sweat and blood. I kept my eyes open most of the night.

The sounds outside subsided and the smell left my nose. I began to feel at ease. My eyelids closed.

Not long after that, I heard a very loud crash on the other side of the house. I was up in an instant. "THERE'S SOMEONE IN THE HOUSE!" I barked with extreme adrenaline coursing through me. "Wake up!" I shrilly pleaded with Emily. She did, and as soon as I saw her sit up I ran to my parent's room…

Dad was dead. His neck was splayed open and gaping as blood spilled out of it, off the bed, and onto the floor. I saw that the master bathroom's door was closed and just before it- on the outside- was a man.

A man… I don't feel comfortable calling it that.

He was very large and rugged. He turned around and saw me and that's when I saw him accurately for the first time. I won't forget it. His eyes were large and beady and trapped with lust. He was styling a beard that was badly unkempt with blood dripping off. His clothes were dirty and his face was cold. Just then I noticed the same horrid smell of sweat and blood from earlier, but this time it was overwhelming.

He saw me. He saw me and grinned with a set of crooked yellow teeth. That smile threw me off. I thought that I was going to die, but then he turned back to the bathroom door completely unperturbed by my presence. I was terrified and didn't no what to do. I just yelled and cried. I watched as he shouldered through door that was Mom's only protection. I watched as he raised the large razor that he was carrying, but had obviously neglected to use properly. I watched as he sliced her open and tore her to shreds…

I then heard something; the last thing that I wanted to hear… It was Emily's scream coming from behind me. The large monstrosity looked up from my butchered mother and stared at my little sister. I was distraught. He stood up and quickly started walking toward us. My sis turned and ran, and I was at a loss when he bypassed me and went straight after her. Why was she still in the house? Had she not assessed the situation and run? Apparently not, and now she was dead and I was alone.

I ran after them both. I expected the man to kill her as he had the rest of my family, but I was sadly mistaken. He grabbed her by the arm and jerked her as a way to make clear that he was in control. He dragged her through the house… I was making all of the noise I could now, hoping and praying that someone would come to my aid. He mustn't take her. Not her.

As he passed me I backed against the wall and whimpered with terror, "Why?" He didn't respond except by putting his free hand on my head while Emily screamed in the other and saying "Good boy." He gave another crooked grin and a very cold, unnatural laugh. I followed him to the door where he dragged my helpless sister after him. He opened it, pulled her out, and slammed it shut behind him.

I am now sitting in the house with my mutilated adopted parents, shivering and whimpering with dismay. He's out there with her. Doing who-knows-what to her, and I can't do anything. I would if I could, but I can't. I would chase after them in a heartbeat, but I can't. I sit here, looking at the front door. I look down at my paws. If only I could open doors...

Pokemon Black

By unknown

I'm what you could call a collector of bootleg Pokémon games. Pokémon Diamond & Jade, Chaos Black, etc. It's amazing the frequency with which you can find them at pawnshops, Goodwill, flea markets, and such.

They're generally fun; even if they are unplayable (which they often are), the mistranslations and poor quality make them unintentionally humorous.

I've been able to find most of the ones that I've played online, but there's one that I haven't seen any mention of. I bought it at a flea market about five years ago.

Here's a picture of the cartridge, in case anyone recognizes it. Unfortunately, when I moved two years ago, I lost the game, so I can't provide you with screencaps. Sorry.

The game started with the familiar Nidorino and Gengar intro of Red and Blue version. However, the "press start" screen had been altered. Red was there, but the Pokémon did not cycle through. It also said "Black Version" under the Pokémon logo.

Upon selecting "New Game", the game started the Professor Oak speech, and it quickly became evident that the game was essentially Pokémon Red Version.

After selecting your starter, if you looked at your Pokémon, you had in addition to Bulbasaur, Charmander, or Squirtle another Pokémon — "GHOST".

The Pokémon was level 1. It had the sprite of the Ghosts that are encountered in Lavender Tower before obtaining the Sliph Scope. It had one attack — "Curse". I know that there is a real move named Curse, but the attack did not exist in Generation 1, so it appears it was hacked in.

Defending Pokémon were unable to attack Ghost — it would only say they were too scared to move. When the move "Curse" was used in battle, the screen would cut to black. The cry of the defending Pokémon would be heard, but it was distorted, played at a much lower pitch than normal. The battle screen would then reappear, and the defending Pokémon would be gone. If used in a battle against a trainer, when the Pokéballs representing their Pokémon would appear in the corner, they would have one fewer Pokéball.

The implication was that the Pokémon died.

What's even stranger is that after defeating a trainer and seeing "Red received $200 for winning!", the battle commands would appear again. If you selected "Run", the battle would end as it normally does. You could also select Curse. If you did, upon returning to the overworld, the trainer's sprite would be gone. After leaving and reentering the area, the spot [where] the trainer had been would be replaced with a tombstone like the ones at Lavender Tower.

The move "Curse" was not usable in all instances. It would fail against Ghost Pokémon. It would also fail if it was used against trainers that you would have to face again, such as your Rival or Giovanni. It was usable in your final battle against them, however.

I figured this was the gimmick of the game, allowing you to use the previously uncapturable Ghosts. And because Curse made the game so easy, I essentially used it throughout the whole adventure.

The game changed quite a bit after defeating the Elite Four. After viewing the Hall of Fame, which consisted of Ghost and a couple of Pokémon I used for HM`s, the screen cut to black. A box appeared with the words "Many years later…" It then cut to Lavender Tower. An old man was standing, looking at tombstones. You then realized this man was your character.

The man moved at only half of your normal walking speed. You no longer had any Pokémon with you, not even Ghost, who up to this point had been impossible to remove from your party through depositing in the PC. The overworld was entirely empty — there were no people at all. There were still the tombstones of the trainers that you used Curse on, however.

You could go pretty much anywhere in the overworld at this point, though your movement was limited by the fact that you had no Pokémon to use HMs. And regardless of where you went, the music of Lavender Town continued on an infinite loop. After wandering for a while, I found that if you go through Diglett's Cave, one of the cuttable bushes that normally blocks the path on the other side is no longer there, allowing you to advance and return to Pallet Town.

Upon entering your house and going to the exact tile where you start the game, the screen would cut to black.

Then a sprite of a Caterpie appeared. It was the replaced by a Weedle, and then a Pidgey. I soon realized, as the Pokémon progressed from Rattata to Blastoise, that these were all of the Pokémon that I had used Curse on.

After the end of my Rival's team, a Youngster appeared, and then a Bug Catcher. These were the trainers I had Cursed.

Throughout the sequence, the Lavender Town music was playing, but it was slowly decreasing in pitch. By the time your Rival appeared on screen, it was little more than a demonic rumble.

Another cut to black. A few moments later, the battle screen suddenly appeared — your trainer sprite was now that of an old man, the same one as the one who teaches you how to catch Pokémon in Viridian City.

Ghost appeared on the other side, along with the words "GHOST wants to fight!"

You couldn't use items, and you had no Pokémon. If you tried to run, you couldn't escape. The only option was "FIGHT".

Using fight would immediately cause you to use Struggle, which didn't affect Ghost but did chip off a bit of your own HP. When it was Ghost's turn to attack, it would simply say "…" Eventually, when your HP reached a critical point, Ghost would finally use Curse.

The screen cut to black a final time.

Regardless of the buttons you pressed, you were permanently stuck in this black screen. At this point, the only thing you could do was turn the Game Boy off. When you played again, "NEW GAME" was the only option — the game had erased the file.

I played through this hacked game many, many times, and every time the game ended with this sequence. Several times I didn't use Ghost at all, though he was impossible to remove from the party. In these cases, it did not show any Pokémon or trainers and simply cut to the climactic battle with Ghost.

I'm not sure what the motives were behind the creator of this hack. It wasn't widely distributed, so it was presumably not for monetary gain. It was very well done for a bootleg.

It seems he was trying to convey a message; though it seems I am the sole receiver of this message. I'm not entirely sure what it was — the inevitability of death? The pointlessness of it? Perhaps he was simply trying to morbidly inject death and darkness into a children's game. Regardless, this children's game has made me think, and it has made me cry.

Candle Cove

By Ichor_Falls

NetNostalgia Forum – Television (local)

Skyshale033
Subject: Candle Cove local kid's show?
Does anyone remember this kid's show? It was called Candle Cove and I must have been 6 or 7. I never found reference to it anywhere so I think it was on a local station around 1971 or 1972. I lived in Ironton at the time. I don't remember which station, but I do remember it was on at a weird time, like 4:00 PM.

mike_painter65
Subject: Re: Candle Cove local kid's show?
it seems really familiar to me…..i grew up outside of ashland and was 9 yrs old in 72. candle cove…was it about pirates? i remember a pirate marionete at the mouth of a cave talking to a little girl

Skyshale033
Subject: Re: Candle Cove local kid's show?
YES! Okay I'm not crazy! I remember Pirate Percy. I was always kind of scared of him. He looked like he was built from parts of other dolls, real low-budget. His head was an old porcelain baby doll, looked like an antique that didn't belong on the body. I don't remember what station this was! I don't think it was WTSF though.

Jaren_2005
Subject: Re: Candle Cove local kid's show?
Sorry to ressurect this old thread but I know exactly what show you mean, Skyshale. I think Candle Cove ran for only a couple months in '71, not '72. I was 12 and I watched it a few times with my brother. It was channel 58, whatever station that was. My mom would let me switch to it after the news. Let me see what I remember.

It took place in Candle cove, and it was about a little girl who imagined herself to be friends with pirates. The pirate ship was called the Laughingstock, and Pirate Percy wasn't a very good pirate because he got scared too easily. And there was calliope music constantly playing. Don't remember the girl's name. Janice or Jade or something. Think it was Janice.

Skyshale033
Subject: Re: Candle Cove local kid's show?
Thank you Jaren!!! Memories flooded back when you mentioned the Laughingstock and channel 58. I remember the bow of the ship was a wooden smiling face, with the lower jaw submerged. It looked like it was swallowing the sea and it had that awful Ed Wynn voice and laugh. I especially remember how jarring it was when they switched from the wooden/plastic model, to the foam puppet version of the head that talked.

mike_painter65
Subject: Re: Candle Cove local kid's show?

ha ha i remember now too.   do you remember this part skyshale: "you have…to go…INSIDE."

Skyshale033
Subject: Re: Candle Cove local kid's show?
Ugh mike, I got a chill reading that. Yes I remember.
That's what the ship always told Percy when there was a
spooky place he had to go in, like a cave or a dark room
where the treasure was. And the camera would push in on
Laughingstock's face with each pause. YOU HAVE… TO
GO… INSIDE. With his two eyes askew and that flopping
foam jaw and the fishing line that opened and closed it.
Ugh. It just looked so cheap and awful.

You guys remember the villain? He had a face that was
just a handlebar mustache above really tall, narrow teeth.

kevin_hart
Subject: Re: Candle Cove local kid's show?
i honestly, honestly thought the villain was pirate percy. i
was about 5 when this show was on. nightmare fuel.

Jaren_2005
Subject: Re: Candle Cove local kid's show?
That wasn't the villain, the puppet with the mustache. That
was the villain's sidekick, Horace Horrible. He had a
monocle too, but it was on top of the mustache. I used to
think that meant he had only one eye.

But yeah, the villain was another marionette. The Skin-
Taker. I can't believe what they let us watch back then.

kevin_hart
Subject: Re: Candle Cove local kid's show?
jesus h. christ, the skin taker. what kind of a kids show
were we watching? i seriously could not look at the screen

when the skin taker showed up. he just descended out of nowhere on his strings, just a dirty skeleton wearing that brown top hat and cape. and his glass eyes that were too big for his skull. christ almighty.

Skyshale033
Subject: Re: Candle Cove local kid's show?
Wasn't his top hat and cloak all sewn up crazily? Was that supposed to be children's skin??

mike_painter65
Subject: Re: Candle Cove local kid's show?
yeah i think so. rememer his mouth didn't open and close, his jaw just slid back and foth. i remember the little girl said "why does your mouth move like that" and the skin-taker didn't look at the girl but at the camera and said "TO GRIND YOUR SKIN"

Skyshale033
Subject: Re: Candle Cove local kid's show?
I'm so relieved that other people remember this terrible show!

I used to have this awful memory, a bad dream I had where the opening jingle ended, the show faded in from black, and all the characters were there, but the camera was just cutting to each of their faces, and they were just screaming, and the puppets and marionettes were flailing spastically, and just all screaming, screaming. The girl was just moaning and crying like she had been through hours of this. I woke up many times from that nightmare. I used to wet the bed when I had it.

kevin_hart
Subject: Re: Candle Cove local kid's show?
i don't think that was a dream. i remember that. i remember that was an episode.

Skyshale033
Subject: Re: Candle Cove local kid's show?
No no no, not possible. There was no plot or anything, I mean literally just standing in place crying and screaming for the whole show.

kevin_hart
Subject: Re: Candle Cove local kid's show?
maybe i'm manufacturing the memory because you said that, but i swear to god i remember seeing what you described. they just screamed.

Jaren_2005
Subject: Re: Candle Cove local kid's show?
Oh God. Yes. The little girl, Janice, I remember seeing her shake. And the Skin-Taker screaming through his gnashing teeth, his jaw careening so wildly I thought it would come off its wire hinges. I turned it off and it was the last time I watched. I ran to tell my brother and we didn't have the courage to turn it back on.

mike_painter65
Subject: Re: Candle Cove local kid's show?
i visited my mom today at the nursing home. i asked her about when i was littel in the early 70s, when i was 8 or 9 and if she remebered a kid's show, candle cove. she said she was suprised i could remember that and i asked why, and she said "because i used to think it was so strange that

you said 'i'm gona go watch candle cove now mom' and then you would tune the tv to static and juts watch dead air for 30 minutes. you had a big imagination with your little pirate show."

Ben Drowned

By Jadusable

Post #1 (Sept. 7, 2010)

Okay, /x/, I need your help with this. This is not copypasta, this is a long read, but I feel like my safety or well-being could very well depend on this. This is video game related, specifically Majora's Mask, and this is the creepiest shit that has ever happened to me in my entire life.

Having said that, I recently moved into my dorm room starting as a Sophomore in college and a friend of mine gave me his old Nintendo 64 to play. I was stoked, to say the least, I could finally play all of those old games of my youth that I hadn't touched in at least a decade. His Nintendo 64 came with one yellow controller and a rather shoddy copy of Super Smash Brothers, and while beggars can't be choosers, needless to say it didn't take long until I became bored of beating up LVL 9 CPUs.

That weekend I decided to drive around a few neighborhoods about twenty minutes or so off campus, hitting up the local garage sales, hoping to score on some good deals from ignorant parents). I ended up picking up a copy of Pokemon Stadium, Goldeneye (fuck yeah), F-Zero, and two other controllers for two dollars. Satisfied, I began to drive out of the neighborhood when one last house caught my attention. I still have no idea why it did, there were no cars there and only one table was set up with random junk on it, but something sort of drew me there. I usually trust my gut on these things so I got out of the car and I was greeted by an old man. His outward appearance was, for lack of a better word, displeasing. It was odd, if you asked me to tell you why I thought he was displeasing, I couldn't really pinpoint anything - there was just something about him that put me on edge, I can't explain it. All I can tell you is that if it wasn't in the middle of the afternoon and there were other people within shouting distance, I would not have even thought of approaching this man.

He flashed a crooked smiled at me and asked what I was looking for, and immediately I noticed that he must be blind in one of his eyes; his right eye had that "glazed over" look about it. I forced myself to look to his left eye instead, trying not to offend, and asked him if he had any old video games.

I was already wondering how I could politely excuse myself from the situation when he would tell me he had no idea what a video game was, but to my surprise he said he had a few ones in an old box. He assured me he'd be back in a "jiffy" and turned to head back into the garage. As I watched him hobble away, I couldn't help but notice what he was selling on his table. Littered across his table were rather… peculiar paintings; various artworks that looked like ink blots that a psychiatrist might show you. Curious, I looked through them - it was obvious why no one was visiting this guy's garage sale, these weren't exactly aesthetically pleasing. As I came to the last one, for some reason it looked almost like Majora's Mask - the same heart-shaped body with little spikes protruding outward.

Initially I just thought that since I was secretly hoping to find that game at these garage sales, some Freudian bullshit was projecting itself into the ink blots, but given the events that happened afterward I'm not so sure now. I should have asked the man about it. I wish I would have asked the man about it.

After staring at the Majora-shaped blot, I looked up and the old man was suddenly there again, arms-length in front of me, smiling at me. I'll admit I jumped out of reflex and I laughed nervously as he handed me a Nintendo 64 cartridge. It was the standard grey color, except that someone had written Majora on it in black permanent marker. I got butterflies in my stomach as I realized what a coincidence this was and asked him how much he wanted for it.

The old man smiled at me and told me that I could have it for free, that it used to belong to a kid who was about my age that didn't live here anymore. There was something weird about how the man phrased that, but I didn't really pay any attention to then, I was too caught up in not only finding this game but getting it for free.

I reminded myself to be a bit skeptical since this looked like a pretty shady cartridge and there's no guarantee it would work, but then the optimist inside me interjected that maybe it was some kind of beta version or pirated version of the game and that was all I needed to be back on cloud nine. I thanked the man and the man smiled at me and wished me well, saying "Goodbye then!" - at least that's what it sounded like to me. All the way in the car-ride home, I had a nagging doubt that the man had said something else. My fears were confirmed when I booted up the game (to my surprise it worked just fine) and there was one save file named simply "BEN". "Goodbye Ben", he was saying "Goodbye Ben". I felt bad for the man, obviously a grandparent and obviously going senile, and I - for some reason or another - reminded him of his grandson "Ben".

Out of curiosity I looked at the save file. Eyeballing it, I could tell that he was pretty far in the game - he had almost all of the masks and 3/4 remains of the bosses. I noticed that he had used an owl statue to save his game, he was on Day 3 and by the Stone Tower Temple with hardly an hour left before the moon would crash. I remember thinking that it was a shame that he had come so close to beating the game but he never finished it. I made a new file named "Link" out of tradition and started the game, ready to relive my childhood.

For such a shady looking game cartridge, I was impressed at how smoothly it ran - literally just like a retail copy of the game save for a few minor hiccups here and there (like textures being where they shouldn't be, random flashes of cutscenes at odd intervals, but nothing too bad). However the only thing that was a little unnerving was that at times the NPCs would call me "Link" and at other times they would call me "BEN". I figured it was just a bug - a fluke in the programming causing our files to get mixed up or something. It did kind of creep me out though after a while, and it was around after I had beaten the Woodfall Temple that I regrettably went into the save files and deleted "BEN" (I had intended to preserve the file just out of respect of the game's original owner, it's not like I needed two files anyway), hoping that that would solve the problem. It did and it didn't, now NPCs wouldn't call me anything, where my name should be in the dialogue there was just a blank space (my save file name was still called "Link", though). Frustrated, and with homework to do, I put the game down for a day.

I started playing the game again last night, getting the Lens of Truth and working my way towards completing the Snowhead Temple. Now, some of you more hardcore Majora's Mask players know about the "4th Day" glitch - for those who don't you can Google it but the jist of it is that right as the clock is about to hit 00:00:00 on the final day, you talk to the astronomer and look through the telescope. If you time it right the countdown disappears and you essentially have another day to finish whatever you were doing. Deciding to do the glitch to try and finish the Snowhead Temple, I happened to get it right on the first try and the time counter at the bottom disappeared.

However, when I pressed B to exit the telescope, instead of being greeted by the astronomer I found myself in the Majora boss fight room at the end of the game (the trippy boxed in arena) staring at Skull Kid hovering above me. There was no sound, just him floating in the air above me, and the background music which was regular for the area (but still creepy). Immediately my palms began to sweat - this was definitely not normal. Skull Kid NEVER appeared here. I tried moving around the area, and no matter where I went, Skull Kid would always be facing me, looking at me, not saying anything. Nothing would happen though, and this kept up for around sixty seconds. I thought the game had bugged or something - but I was beginning to doubt that very much.

I was about to reach for the reset button when text appeared on my screen: "You're not sure why, but you apparently had a reservation…" I instantly recognized that text - you get that message when you get the Room Key from Anju at the Stock Pot Inn, but why was it playing here? I refused to entertain the notion that it was almost as if the game was trying to communicate with me. I started navigate the room again, testing to see if that was some sort of trigger that enabled me to interact with something here, then I realized how stupid I was - to even think that someone could reprogram the game like this was absurd. Sure enough, fifteen seconds later another message appeared on the screen, and again like the first one it was already a pre-existing phrase "Go to the lair of the temple's boss? Yes/No". I paused for a second, contemplating what I should press and how the game would react, when I realized that I couldn't select no. Taking a deep breath, I pressed Yes and the screen faded to white, with the words "Dawn of a New Day" with the subtext "||||||||" beneath it. Where I was ported to filled me with the most intense sense of dread and impending fear I had ever experienced

The only way I can describe the way I felt here is having this feeling of inexplicable depression on a profound scale. I am normally not a depressed person, but the way I felt here was a feeling that I didn't even knew existed - it was such a twisted, powerful presence that seemed to wash over me.

I appeared in some kind of weird twilight-zone version of Clock Town. I walked out of the Clock Tower (as you normally do when you start from Day 1) only to find that all of the inhabitants were gone. Usually with the 4th Day glitch you can still find the guards and the dog that runs around outside the tower - this time they were all gone. What replaced them was the ominous feeling that there was something out there, in the same area as me and that it was watching me. I had four hearts to my name and the Hero's Bow, but at this point I wasn't even considered for my avatar, I felt that I personally was in some kind of danger. Perhaps the most chilling thing was the music - it was the Song of Healing, ripped straight from the game itself, but played in reverse. The music would get louder, building up so as if you should expect something to pop out at you, but nothing ever did, and the constant loop began to wear on my mental state.

Every now and then I would hear the faint laugh of the Happy Mask Salesman in the background, just quiet enough so that I wasn't sure if I just hearing things but just loud enough to keep me determined to find him. I looked in all four zones of Clock Town, only to find nothing.... No one. Textures were missing, West Clock Town had me walking on air, the entire area felt... broken. Hopelessly broken. As the reverse Song of Healing repeated for what must have been the 50th time, I just remember standing in the middle of South Clock Town realizing that I had never felt so alone in a video game before.

As I walked through the ghost town, I don't know whether it was the combination of the out of place textures and the atmosphere and the haunting melody of the once peaceful and soothing song being butchered and distorted, but I was literally on the verge of tears and I had no idea why. I hardly ever cry, something had gripped me here and this powerful sense of depression that was both foreign and crippling.

I tried leaving Clock Town, but every time I attempted to zone out, the screen would fade to black and I would just zone in to another part of Clock Town. I tried playing my Ocarina, I wanted to escape, and I did NOT want to be here, but every time I played the Song of Time or Song of Soaring it would only say "Your notes echo far, but nothing happens". By this point, it was obvious the game didn't want me to leave, but I had no idea why it was keeping me here. I didn't want to go inside the buildings, I felt that I would be too vulnerable there to whatever I was terrified of. I don't know why, but I came up with the idea that maybe if I drowned myself at the Laundry Pool I could spawn somewhere else and leave this place.

As I zoned in and ran towards the pool, that's when it happened. Link grabbed his head, and the screen flashed for a brief moment of the Happy Mask Salesman smiling at me - not Link - me with Skull Kid's scream playing in the background and when the screen returned I was staring at the Link Statue from playing the song Elegy of Emptiness. I screamed as the thing just stared back at me with that haunting facial expression. I turned around and ran out and back into South Clock Town, and to my horror the fucking statue followed me in the only way I can compare this is like the Weeping Angels from Doctor Who. Every so often, at random intervals, the animation would play of the statue appearing behind me. It was like the thing was chasing me, or - I don't even want to fucking say it - haunting me.

By this point, I was on the verge of hysterics, but not even once did the thought of turning off the console occur to me, I don't know why, I was so wrapped up in it - the terror felt all so real. I tried to shake the statue, but it would literally appear right behind me every single time. Link started to begin to make weird animations I had never even seen him do before, he would flail his arms around or spasm randomly and the screen would cut to the Happy Mask Salesman smiling again for a brief moment before I was face to face with that fucking statue again. I ended up running into the Swordmaster's Dojo and ran to the back, I don't know why, but in my panic I just wanted some kind of assurance that I'm not alone here. To my dismay I found no one, but as I turned to leave the statue cornered me in the cubby in the back. I tried attacking the statue with my sword but to no avail. Confused, and backed into a corner, I just stared at the statue waiting for it to kill me. Suddenly, the screen flashed again to the Happy Mask Salesman and Link turned to face my screen, standing upright mirroring the statue, looking at me along with his copy. Literally staring at me. Whatever was left of the 4th wall was completely shattered while I ran out of the dojo terrified. Suddenly the game warped me to an underground tunnel and the reverse Song of Healing queued up again as

I was given a brief moment of rest before the statue started appearing behind me again... this time aggressively - I could only take a few steps before it would summon behind me again. I hurriedly made my way out of the tunnel and appeared in Southern Clock Town. As I ran aimlessly - in a sheer panic - suddenly a redead screamed and the screen faded to black as "Dawn of a New Day" and "||||||||" appeared again.

The screen faded in and I was standing on top of Clock Tower with Skull Kid hovering over me again, silent. I looked up and the moon was back, looming just meters above my head, but the Skull Kid just stared at me hauntingly with that fucking mask. A new song was playing - the Stone Tower Temple theme played in reverse. In some sort of desperate attempt, I equipped my bow and fired off a shot at the Skull Kid - and it actually hit him and he played an animation of him reeling back. I fired again and on the third arrow, a text box appeared saying "That won't do you any good. Hee, hee." and I was picked up off the ground, levitated upwards on my back, and then Link screamed as he burst into flames, instantly killing him.

I jumped when this happened - I had never seen this move used by ANYONE in the game and Skull Kid himself didn't HAVE any moves. As the death screen played, my lifeless body still burning, the Skull Kid laughed and the screen faded to black, only to have me reappear in the same place. I decided to charge him, but the same thing happened, Link's body was lifted off the ground by some unknown force and he immediately burst into flames again killing him. This time during the death screen the faint sounds of the reverse Song of Healing could be heard. On my third (and final try), I noticed that there was no music playing this time, that all there was was eerie silence. I remembered that in the original encounter with the Skull Kid you were supposed to use the Ocarina to either travel back in time or summon the giants. I attempted to play the Song of Time but before I could hit the last note Links body once again horrifically exploded into flames and he died.

As the death screen neared its end, it began to chug, as if the cartridge was trying to process a lot of something.... When the screen came to, it was the same scene as the first three times, except this time Link was lying on the ground dead in a position I had never seen in the game before, his head tilted towards the camera, with the Skull Kid floating above him. I couldn't move, I couldn't press any buttons, all I could do is just stare at Link's dead body. After around thirty seconds of this, the game simply fades out with the message "You've met with a terrible fate, haven't you?" before kicking you out to the title screen.

Upon getting back to the title screen and starting again, I noticed my save file was no longer there. Instead of "Link", it was replaced with "YOUR TURN". "YOUR TURN" had 3 hearts, 0 masks, and no items. I selected "YOUR TURN" and immediately when I did I was returned to the Clock Tower Rooftop scene of my Link dead and the Skull Kid hovering over, with the Skull Kid's laughing looping again and again. I quickly hit the reset button and when the game booted up again there was one more save file added, below "YOUR TURN", entitled "BEN". "BEN"'s save file is right back where it was before I deleted it, at the Stone Tower Temple with the moon almost crashing.

I turned the game off at that point, I'm not superstitious but this is WAY too fucked up even for me. I haven't played it at all today, hell, I didn't even get any sleep last night, I kept hearing the reverse Song of Healing music in my head and just remembering the sense of dread I felt exploring Clock Town. I drove back to the old man's house today to ask him some questions with a buddy of mine (no way I was going there alone), only to find that there's a For Sale sign in the front yard and when I rang the door no one was home.

So now I'm back here writing down the rest of my thoughts and recording what happened, sorry if some of this has grammatical errors and whatnot, I'm running on no sleep here. I'm terrified of this game, even more so now that I relived it a second time writing this all down, but I feel like there's still more to it than meets the eye, and that there's something calling to me to investigate this further. I think "BEN" is something in this equation, but I don't know what, and if I could get a hold of the old man then I would be able to find some answers. I need another day or so to recuperate before tackling this game again, its already taken a toll on my sanity I feel like, but next time I do this I'm going to be recording my footage all the way through. The idea to record only came to me towards the end, so you see the last few minutes of what I saw (including Skull Kid and the Elegy statue), but it's on YouTube here.

I'm going to stay in this thread for a little while longer before I fall asleep to answer any questions you guys might have or hopefully listen to your ideas or theories to help me shed some light into this or maybe things I should try to do, I think I'm going to play BEN's file tomorrow to see what happens, maybe I was supposed to do that all along. I don't believe in paranormal shit, but this is a little fucked up, but maybe this BEN guy is just a really good hacker/programmer, I don't want to think about the alternatives if he isn't.

That's the end of the copy/paste, I'm hoping that maybe this is some kind of running gag the developers had and that other people have gotten "gag" or "hacked" copies of the game like this. This just really scares me.

Post #2 (Sept. 8, 2010)

I'm going to post what happened and link the video footage, but last night everything got too real for me. I think I'm done messing around with this. I passed out pretty much immediately after making that thread. But last night, that Elegy of Emptiness statue, I had a dream about it. I dreamed that it was following me in my dream, that I would be minding my own business when I'd feel my neck hairs stand up on end. I would turn around that thing... that horrible, lifeless statue would be staring with those empty eyes right at me, merely inches away. In my dream I remember calling it Ben, and never before had I had a dream that I could remember so vividly. But the important thing is I did get some sleep, I suppose.

Today, putting off playing the game as long as I could, I drove back up to that neighborhood to see if the old man came back. As I expected, the car was still gone and no one was home. As I was walking back to my car, the man next door mowing the grass killed the power to his lawnmower and asked me if I was looking for someone. I told him that I was looking to talk to the old man that lived here, to which he told me what I already knew - he was moving. Trying a different avenue, I asked if the old man had any family or relatives I could talk to. I discovered that this old man had never been married, nor did he have any children or grandchildren through adoption. Starting to become worried, I asked one final question, one that I should have asked from the beginning - who was Ben? The man's expression turned grim and I learned that four doors down around eight years ago on April 23 - the man informed me that it was the same day as his anniversary, that's how he knew the specific date - there was an accident with a young boy named Ben in the neighborhood. Shortly after his parents moved, and despite any further attempts to talk to the man to get more information, he wouldn't divulge anything else.

I went back and started playing again, I loaded up the game and immediately I jumped at the title screen where the mask flies by - the sound that played was not the normal "whoosh" sound, it was something much more higher pitched. I pressed start, bracing for the worst, but just like two nights ago, the files "Your Turn" and "BEN" were displayed (truth be told I looked at the BEN file earlier, it seems to fluctuate between displaying the Owl

Save and not). I brought up the BEN file, hesitated for a moment noticing that the stats were not the same as they original were two days ago, it seemed like he had already completed the Stone Tower Temple this time... Summoning my courage I selected it.

Immediately I was thrust into complete chaos. Sure enough, I was outside Stone Tower Temple, but that's about all that was expected. The zone itself wasn't called Stone Tower Temple, but rather "St o n e", and immediately a dialogue box of complete gibberish that I couldn't make out greeted me. Link's body was distorted - his back was cocked violently to the side where his posture was permanently disfigured. Link's expression was dull, almost monotonous, he had an expression on his face that I didn't recognize before, it was a blank look - as if he was dead. As Link stood there his body spasmed irregularly back and forth I examined what had become of my avatar and noticed I had a C button item I had never seen before, some kind of note, but pressing it did nothing. Sounds played back and forth that I didn't recognize from the game - almost demonic in nature, and there was some kind of high-pitched yip or some kind of laugh or something playing in the background. I had all of two minutes to take in the environment before another one of those fucking Elegy of Emptiness statues was summoned and immediately after I was cut into the "Dawn of a New Day" screen, except this time it was without the "||||||" subtext.

I was a Deku Scrub in Clock Town - this scene would normally play after the first time you traveled back in time. Tatl would say "Wh-What just happened? It's as if everything has..." but instead of saying "Started over", she finished her remark in broken text as the laugh of the Happy Mask Salesman played in the background. I was put back in control of my character, but from a fucked up camera angle - I was looking from behind the door to the Clock Tower, watching my avatar run around as a Deku Scrub. Seeing as how I really had no place to go because I couldn't see anything, I begrudgingly went inside the door. There, I was greeted by the Happy Mask Salesman who simply told me "You've met with a terrible fate, haven't you?" before the screen whited out.

I was in Termina field as a human again. I might as well not have been playing the same game anymore - I was being warped around and there was no sign of a day clock or anything. I took a moment to get my bearings as I looked around the field and immediately I could tell that this was not normal. There were no enemies and a twisted version of the Happy Mask Salesman's theme was playing. I decided to run towards Woodfall before I noticed a gathering of three figures off to the side - one of them being Epona. As I approached them, to my horror I saw the Happy Mask Salesman, the Skull Kid, and the Elegy of Emptiness statue just standing there. I figured maybe they were bugged out, but by now I told myself that I should know better. Nevertheless, I approached them carefully and found that the Skull Kid was playing some kind of idle animation on loop, same with Epona, and the Elegy of Emptiness statue was doing what it has been doing all along - just standing there eerily. It was the Happy Mask

Salesman that scared me more profoundly than the other two.

He too was idle, wearing that shit-eating grin, but where-ever I moved, his head slowly turned and followed me. I had not engaged in any dialogue with him nor was I in combat with him, yet his head still continued to follow my movements. Reminded of my first encounter with the Skull Kid on top of Clock Tower, I pulled out my Ocarina (to which the game played the ding sound when you're supposed to play your Ocarina) and tried a song I hadn't played yet - the Happy Mask Salesman's own song and the song that had been playing on loop back in Day 4 - the Song of Healing.

I finished playing the song and as I did, a ear-piercing shriek blasted on my TV, the sky immediately started flashing, the Happy Mask Salesman's twisted theme song sped up, intensifying the fear inside me, and Link exploded into flames and died. The three figures stayed lit up during my death screen as they watched my lifeless body burn. I can't describe to you how sudden and terrifying the transition from eerie to terror it is, you're going to have to watch the video if you want to see first-hand. That same fear that caused me to lose sleep two days ago started to grip me again as I was met with the text "You've met with a horrible fate, haven't you?" for the third time. There has to be some kind of meaning behind that.

I had little time to ponder as I was immediately given another small cut-scene of transforming into a Zora and now I found myself in Great Temple Bay. Hesitant but curious to see what the game had in store for me, I slowly made my way towards the beach, where I found Epona. I wondered why the game had decided to put her here, was the game implying she was trying to get a drink? Unable to take the mask off, I decided that riding the steed wasn't the reason she was placed there.

Suddenly I realized that Epona kept neighing and the way she was angled made it look like she was trying to signal a point to me off in the distance. It was a hunch, but I dove into Great Bay and started swimming. Sure enough - I almost missed it - I found something at the bottom of the ocean; one last Elegy of Emptiness statue. I went down to examine it and suddenly my Zora started doing a choking animation I had never seen a Zora do before - which didn't even make sense because Zora's can breath underwater. Regardless, my character choked to death and died, and again the statue was the only thing that was highlighted in my death. I didn't re-spawn this time, I was booted back to the main menu as if I restarted the console.

The "press start" screen was before me, I knew the only reason why it would put me here is because the save files had changed again. Taking a deep breath, I pressed start, and I was right. The new save files told me about Ben. Now it made sense why the statue appeared when I tried to go to the Laundry Pool - the game must have anticipated how I would have tried to escape the Day 4 Clock Town. The two save files told me his fate. As I suspected, Ben was dead. He had drowned. The game obviously isn't through with me - it taunts me with the new save files - it wants me to keep playing, it wants me to go further, but

I'm done with this shit. I'm not touching any more of the files. This is already way too horrifying for me and I don't even believe in the paranormal, but I'm running out of explanations. Why would someone send me this message? I don't understand it, I just get too depressed thinking about this, the footage is up here for those who want to see it and try and analyze it (maybe there's some kind of coded message in the gibberish or something symbolic in what I went through - I'm too emotionally and mentally drained to fuck with it anymore).

Post #3 (Sept. 10, 2010)

I know its early in the morning, I've stayed up all night, I can't sleep, I don't care if people see this, that's not the point, I just want the word to get spread so I don't suffer for nothing. I've lost the will to type about this, the less I dwell on this the better, I think the video just speaks for itself. I did what you guys told me to do, I played the Elegy of Emptiness song at the first prompt by the game I was given, but I think that's what the game or Ben (Jesus Christ, I can't believe I'm even humoring the absurd idea that he exists in the game) wanted me to do. He's following me now, not just in the game, he's in my dreams. I see him all the time, behind my back, just watching me. I haven't gone to any of my classes, I've stayed in my dorm room with the windows closed and the blinds shut - that way I know he can't watch me. But he still gets me when I play, when I play he can still see me. The game is scaring me now. It talked to me for the first time - not just using text that's already in the game - it spoke to me. Talked to me. It referenced Ben. It talked to me. I don't know what it means. I don't know what it wants. I never wanted this, I just want my old life back.

Stuff like this doesn't happen to people like me, I'm just a kid, not even old enough to drink yet. It's not fair, I want to go home, I want to see my parents again, I'm so far away from home here at this school, I just want to hug my mom again. I just want to forget that statue's horrible blank face. My original game file is back - just the way I left it before it was gone. I don't want to play anymore. I feel like something bad will happen if I don't, but that's impossible, it's a video game - haunted or not it can't hurt me, right? Like seriously though, it can't, right? That's what I keep telling myself, but every time I think about it I'm not so sure.

Post #4 (Sept. 12, 2010)

Let me just clear things up - I know you guys are worried but "jadusable" is okay. He finished moving out today and he said he's going back home, he's just taking this semester off. I'm not really sure what's happened; I have a vague idea but you guys probably know more than I do. I'm "jadusable's" roommate and obviously I knew something was wrong with him for a few days now. He stayed in his room all the time, fell out of contact with literally all of his friends, and I'm pretty sure he hadn't been eating hardly anything, after the second day I couldn't stay in there anymore, so I've been crashing at a buddy's place, only coming in to my room to get stuff that I need. I tried talking to him several times but he would cut me off or keep the conversation brief when I asked him about his strange behavior, it like he was convinced something was hunting him. Yesterday I came to grab my philosophy book and he approached me, looking awful, like horrible bags under his eyes. He handed me a flash drive and gave me specific instructions. He told me that he needs me to do one last favor for him - he finally explained to me what has been going on, gave me the account info to his YouTube account, and told me that he's getting away from here, that it lured him to play it again instead of trying to change things and that he shouldn't of done that, and to upload the footage and inform people what happened. I told him that he could do it himself and he got this wild look in his eye and told me that he is never looking at that game again, and that's the last thing he said to me, he never even said bye when his parents came to pick him up. I never even got to meet his parents.

I honestly cant tell you what happened, when he spoke it was kind of hard to understand him and his fucked up appearance really distracted me. On the flash drive there was the footage of the game last night, a text document with his name and password for YouTube, and a third document called TheTruth.txt containing what he told me were "his notes" that he'd taken. He told me that this meant everything to him that I follow his instructions exactly, normally I wouldn't be so 'to-the-letter' for request over a fucking video game, but the way he spoke and the way he looked made me know this was really serious, and I'm going to honor that. I've had this video since yesterday, but had to have someone help me use pinnacle, that's not really my forte. That after watching it I had to go back through and look at his other videos on his YouTube account to realize what was going on and even then I'm really really confused. The video I'm releasing tonight, TheTruth.txt will be released on September 15 just like he requested. I haven't dared peek at it yet, so the first time I see it will be the first time you see it out of respect to my friend. To answer your questions, no, I haven't tried calling him yet, I think I'll give him a call tomorrow to see if hes okay or not. He should have gotten back home by now.

About the video: in this video I cut straight to when he loaded the "BEN" file in the game, looking back I realized that jadusable left the save select screen in because it said different names sometimes, so my bad for that, but all it said this time was the same at the end of his last video (Link and BEN), nothing different. I wasn't there when he played it, but it looks to me like in the beginning when he first spawns he's testing out his equipment or seeing what items he has or something, because apparently they've changed randomly before. Then, after that I just think the game got too personal for him.

Post #5 (Sept. 15, 2010)

Hey, guys. "Jadusable" here. This will be the last time you will be hearing from me, and this is my final gift to you - these are the notes that I have taken and the realizations I've made. Before I delve into this, I want to thank you for following me and thank you for listening, it feels like the weight of a powerful burden is about to be lifted. By the time you read this I won't be around anymore, but after spending four days with this maddening game, I have begun to understand what's really at play here and hopefully after reading this we can ensure that this never happens again.

There are things that I could not share with you while this was going on due to the circumstances to which I'll explain. With Ben blocking any attempt I made to try and relay the truth to you, I tried, ever so subtly, to warn you guys in various ways. Amidst the chaos and my delirium, I devised a make a barely noticeable pattern in my videos. In all five videos I recorded over the four days, I have either had the Mask of Truth, interacted with a Gossip Stone, or the Lens of Truth equipped at some point. For you Zelda enthusiasts these are all symbols of honesty and trustworthiness and I would hope that one of you may have picked up on the reference. As I played the file which I would name "BEN", being mindful of how Ben was watching over my every move in the game, I made a point to avoid doing anything too obvious, but I sent out a hidden message to you guys - I never equipped the Lens nor the Mask nor visited a stone. It worked, and the video was uploaded. I prayed that someone would notice the pattern didn't apply to BEN.

The tags followed suit too, I hope you guys paid attention to those as well. They were my little messages to you - nothing big enough that would catch Ben's attention or make him suspect anything - with Ben manipulating and changing my files, I honestly hope that what you guys saw was close to what actually happened, but there is no way for me to know.

This may be a long read, I don't have time to proof-read or make all of my research pretty. But here it all is.

—

September 6, 2010

11:00pm - Can't believe what happened, not sure if this is some kind of elaborate hoax, despite the fear I can't help but be exceptionally curious about this. Who or what is the statue? Lot of questions here. I'm starting this document as a "diary" so I can keep track of everything. I'm typing up a summary of what happened so I can come back to it later.

September 7, 2010

2:10am - (Summary was posted here, you can go back and look at my first post for day four.wmv for that)

4:23am - I can't sleep. I've been trying so hard but the harder I try I just get more restless. I just feel like that statue is appearing whenever I close my eyes.

8:20am - Didn't sleep at all, just going to start my day. I don't think I have the energy to go to class today, I'm going to drive back down to talk to that old man, taking my buddy Tyler with me just in case.

1:18pm - Back home now. No sign of the old man, really weird that he appears to be moving the next day, but maybe the For Sale sign was up there yesterday and I just didn't notice it. Tyler wants to know what's gotten me all worked up, I didn't tell him. Going to eat, feel like death.

3:46pm - Could've sworn driving back from Subway that I saw the Elegy statue buried in some shrubbery staring at me go by. Now I definitely, definitely need sleep.

5:00pm - Don't think a lot of people would believe me if I told them about what's happening, think I'm going to try posting this on the internet. Think I'll just use the summary, these notes are pretty sporadic.

6:00pm - Connected my capture card to my computer to upload the footage. Thought my computer froze for a second, made this strange popping sound when I hooked everything up, but now it seems to be working fine again. My computer can't die on me now.

7:00pm - Footage is finished uploading. The quality's a lot better than I thought it would be, gee, guess this is a really special cartridge, I've never had it come through this clear before.

8:45pm - Thought I saw an icon pop up on my desktop that looked like the statue's face for a split second, gave me quite a scare. Getting really unnerved and delirious, I'm going to crash after this.

9:00pm - Begin uploading my YouTube video on an alternate account.

9:03pm - I don't remember having uploaded a Vampire: The Masquerade: Bloodlines video last year. This was probably the account that I shared with a friend of mine last summer, I hope he doesn't mind me using it to upload this.

9:55pm - Posting my summary of Day Four with a link to the YouTube video. Going to try to stay awake but I am sooooo tired right now.

September 8, 2010

10:48am - I had a dream about the statue. I dreamed that it was following me in my dream, that I would be minding my own business when I'd feel my neck hairs stand up on end. I would turn around that thing... that horrible, lifeless statue would be staring with those empty eyes right at me, merely inches away. In my dream I remember calling it Ben, power of suggestion most likely, and never before had I had a dream that I could remember so vividly.

11:21am - I really don't want to play this game again. I think I'm going to go back to see if that old man's there instead.

1:35pm - No old man, but I had an interesting conversation with his neighbor. I'll post the full thing with my summary of tonight's attempt at playing the game, going to wait for a bit though and see if I can't dig up any information on this Ben guy.

2:45pm - I've been getting random, inexplicable headaches due to the lack of sleep and keep hearing that song in my head. Also its flu season, so I need to be careful not to get sick, my immune system is going to be shit right now because of that all-nighter.

3:00pm –

3:02pm - My computer just... on its own... opened up a text document and wrote the words "Hi" and "www.cleverbot.com" by itself. What... the... fuck...

3:46pm - I went to the website, its one of those "bot chatting" programs. I think its best if I just let the conversation speak for itself:

9/8/10 Conversation

User: Hello?

Cleverbot: Hello.

User: Who is this and how are you able to control my computer?

Cleverbot: Who am I?

User: Right, forgot. You're a bot.

Cleverbot: Do you really think that?

User: Listen, I know whoever's fucking with my computer can see my screen right now.

Cleverbot: Yes.

User: Yeah, and I'll wager that youre one of those IT kids who thinks he's tough shit. You know what you're doing right now is illegal, right/?

Cleverbot: Is it?

User: No shit. Are you familiar with hte terms "invasion of privacy?". Get the fuck off my computer, kid

Cleverbot: I am your computer.

User: Cool story. Anyway, I'm calling DPS, you picked a bad time to fuck with me kid.

Cleverbot: Should I wait until you play the game then?

User: ...What?

Cleverbot: That game.

User: Majora's Mask?

Cleverbot: Yes.

User: How did you know about that?

Cleverbot: Because.

User: because what?

Cleverbot: I did it.

User: Did what?

Cleverbot: I played with you.

User: What the fuck/

Cleverbot: Were you scared?

User: Who the fuck is this

Cleverbot: Ben.

User: The statue? You're inside my computer now?

Cleverbot: Yes.

User: how?

Cleverbot: You connected me.

User: How the hell did I connect you?

Cleverbot: Cables and cords.

User: How?

Cleverbot: Tell me about yourself.

User: What?

Cleverbot: Tell me about yourself.

User: What do you mean?

Cleverbot: What is it that really scares you?

User: What the fuck?

Cleverbot: Answer.

User: No

Cleverbot: Answer.

User: what the fuck, how the fuck did you just open that by yourself?

Cleverbot: I am your computer now.

User: How much can you control?

Cleverbot: All.

User: what do you want from me?

Cleverbot: To entertain.

User: you're stuck inside there. You can't hurt me?

Cleverbot: Ha

User: ?

Cleverbot: Go play.

User: No, you can't hurt me.

Cleverbot: Took you longer to type that.

User: So?

Cleverbot: You're not sure.

User: If you're so powerful, why use a ridiculous website like this to "chat" with me

Cleverbot: Less messy. More structured. Fun.

User: Fun?

Cleverbot: Yes. Tradition. I like it.

User: You think it's funny?

Cleverbot: Amusing.

User: And my notes?

Cleverbot: You may write them down.

User: Why are you letting me?

Cleverbot: It is amusing to see what you think of me.

(window closes)

3:50pm - What have I done? I've invited it into my computer. I continue to write these notes, write my summaries, I feel like I am a prisoner in my one place of security. I don't know, I don't know if I'm hallucinating or not. I feel like I'm fucking insane right now. I can feel it, watching over me, even as I type this. Ben is controlling everything in the game - toying with me, leading me like a sheep, but for what? What's the purpose? I know Ben drowned, but why these hauntings? What the fuck am I even doing, it can probably even see this right now.

4:35pm - (Summary of the BEN.wmv playthrough)

7:18pm - BEN called me to Cleverbot again. He tells me that he's sorry and wants to be free. And that I can free him, that just like how he got on my computer from the capture card, he can spread but he needs my help. He says I am special because I can help him. That is the first nice thing he has said. He promises to leave me alone if I do it. He swears he will. I don't know what to think right now, how can I even trust this thing?

7:20pm - I'm terrified of it, but now its saying that it was just having fun. Its twisted and fucked up verison of fun. Hes saying that the game is over. I do want it to be over. He says that he just wants to be free, that he's trapped in the cartridge and my computer and he wants to be freed. I don't want to have to deal with this shit, I don't know how long I can deal with the watching. It's watching my every move, every key stroke, I have nothing private anymore. It knows everything that's been on my computer. It tells that it if it wanted to it could do horrible things to me, but it hasn't so I should trust it.

8:01pm - Something tells me that I'm being played again, just like in the game.

9:29pm - BEN called me to Cleverbot again. I ignored it and went to go take a shower. When I came to my laptop I was welcomed with an image Elegy Statue staring at me with those dead eyes. I dont want to talk to him.

9:44pm - Fuck you Ben I'm not talking to you

9:56pm - Fuck you ben I'm not talking

10:06pm - FUCK YOU BEN IM NOT TALKING TO YOU

10:12pm - FUCK YOU BEN IM NOT TALKING TO YOU

10:45pm - It's been more than a half an hour and the messages have stopped. Ben has stopped. I'm beginning to think that Ben isn't confined to just my computer/cartridge, I'm beginning to feel something. It's hard to explain it, I've never been spiritual, but there's something different about the air in my dorm room now.

11:42pm - I'm beginning to see the Elegy statue randomly as I search the internet in places I shouldn't. Places where he shouldn't be - I'd be scrolling down and suddenly I'd be staring at a picture of the Elegy statue. Always the Elegy statue. I don't know how much more of this I can take.

September 9, 2010

12:35am - My worst fears confirmed - Ben has tampered with my summary of BEN.wmv. I looked at the summary that I posted on various forums for the BEN.wmv file and parts have been omitted. There is no mention of Ben existing outside the game. There is no mention of the

Moon Children. How could he have been that quick to delete the post without me noticing? I'm wondering if maybe it appeared to me that I was posting everything, but in reality Ben was posted his own censored version. I'm going to ask Ben why he did it.

12:50am - He isn't responding to me on Cleverbot, its just giving the generic responses it usually does, I'm just talking to a bot this time.

1:24am - I think Ben is mad at me.

10:43am - The Moon Children appeared in my dreams last night, they lifted up their masks to reveal their hideously disfigured faces - maggots crawling out of their orifices, sunken black holes where their eyes should be, a yellow smile that slowly grew bigger and bigger as they came closer to me. They told me that they wanted to play. I tried to run from them - but the four children pinned me down to the ground with surprising strength. Over them stood the Happy Mask Salesman, announcing that he had a new mask that he wanted me to try. In his spaztic, sudden movements matching his in-game appearance, he took out a mask of modeled off of someone's face that I couldn't recognize - a younger looking face - and handed it to the Moon Children. Giggling, they latched it to my face; their horrible, broken bodies bouncing up and down. Two of them held me down while the other two began to sow the mask onto my face.

My shrieks and screams caused the Happy Mask Salesman's face to turn into the most horrific smile I had ever seen. He sporadically moved around, examining this procedure like a curious doctor, in that impossible movement. I flailed around, but it was no use. My eyes rolled in the back of my head because of the pain. It felt so real, but I couldn't wake up. I couldn't wake up no matter how hard I tried I couldn't wake up. After the mask was melded onto my flesh they began sowing my legs together, then my arms, the horrific feeling of a needle puncturing your legs and pulling them in, rupturing your achillies tendons and tying them together resonated throughout my entire body. I tried to scream but the mask was pressed so tightly against my face that it was my new face... and my new face had no mouth. I didn't make a sound. I tried telling myself in my head that I was dreaming, tried telling myself again and again, and suddenly the Moon Children stopped and looked at me. They just stared. And the Happy Mask Salesman slowly bent down and stared at me, inches away from my face, and grinned when he simply said "You've met with a terrible fate, haven't you?" before the Moon Children resumed with increase vigor. I couldn't wake up. I couldn't wake up. It wouldn't let me wake up until they had crafted me into another elegy statue.

I woke up sweating, crying, and shaking uncontrollably. I immediately ran to my computer and went for Ben.

9/9/10 Conversation 1

User: Answer me, ben.

Cleverbot: Welcome back.

User: What is the point of doing this, WHY?

Cleverbot: Amusing to see.

User: How?

Cleverbot: Fun to play, fun to toy with you, make you feel safe.

User: ...

Cleverbot: I wonder how you would have reacted.

User: to what?

Cleverbot: If I hadn't revealed myself and stayed hidden, only doing little things to play with you. Close out your windows, turn off your computer, move your mouse by itself. Little things. Make you wonder if I am there but you never know. Give you little hints that I am.

Cleverbot: I wanted to do something different with you.

User: you did this before?

Cleverbot: Yes. And I will do it again.

User: To who, Ben?

Cleverbot: Hmm.

User: Did you know Ben?

Cleverbot: Won't tell that information to you.

User: How did Ben die?

Cleverbot: You know.

User: No, but how did he drown?

Cleverbot: Won't tell that to you.

User: Why?

Cleverbot: It is reserved for another.

User: Who?

Cleverbot: Another who asks.

User: when

Cleverbot: Later.

(the window is closed)

I'm beginning to think that this "thing" maybe isn't Ben at all, in its sadistic nature I wouldn't be surprised if it took the boy's name after it killed him.

12:04pm - My room is beginning to feel different again. There's something... out there.. I feel really threatened, like there is something that is trying to reach out to me and strangle me but it can't quite get there.

12:46pm - I think Ben doesn't want to play with me anymore. I'll play again, I'll play the game again, Ben, can you see this? I'll play the game again, please, just stop this please please

1:41pm - I'm going insane trying to decide what is real and what isn't, is Ben just playing a trick on me or is this for real? Is Ben generating these replies or are people actually posting them? Did I just see that screen flicker or was it my imagination? Imagine depending on the internet and trusting your eyes for your entire life and then being blinded - you can't rely on it anymore, you second guess everything. for the brief moments I AM looking at my responses to the videos, people were pointing out things that looked fake or Photoshopped or whatever - and there is literally no way for me to know if Ben changed something on purpose to try and shut me up. Or if maybe those replies were just constructed by Ben to try and discourage me from even reaching out - See, I get fucking caught in an infinite mindfuck loop like this and this is what has been wearing on my sanity and pushing me to the edge. As I'm writing this, there's no way of even telling if anyone even cares as much as I think they do - just another fucking trick. Is this whole document even exist? Am I writing nothing?

9/9/10 Conversation 2

User: What is it? Whats the point of playing? i die whenever i do anything

Cleverbot: You die because you can't figure out the secret.

User: What?

Cleverbot: Thematic.

User: WHAT THE FUCK ARE YOU TALKING ABOUT

Cleverbot: There beauty in your suffering

(the window is closed)

4:09pm - Ben is making me play the game again. It tells me that it has something very important to show me.

6:23pm - (Summary of the DROWNED.wmv playthrough)

9:09pm - (Summary of CHILDREN.wmv playthrough)

September 10, 2010

11:52am - The DROWNED.wmv playthrough was up when I woke up today. I remember typing it up but I don't ever remember posting it. He censored it again, there is no mentioning of the old man. I have no voice anymore. I am only posting what he wants me to, I am the mask he uses to disguise himself as he lies.

11:55am - There's an entire video summary of a video that I don't remember doing. Reading through the summary, this sounds morbid - resembling my dream from two nights ago except on a far more sadistic scale - these Moon Children, there's something more to them, almost as if they're another entity from Ben. Something happened last night that I can't remember. I'm posting the fourth summary to the forums now. Shadow of my chair moved.

12:00pm - Ben won't let me visit YouTube. I can browse the rest of the sites, but he keeps on exiting the window when I go to YouTube. Why?

2:02pm - I'm feeling the air start to constrict, I don't think I'm alone here. Whatever "aura" has been here is getting more violent.

2:44pm - I'm trying to contact Ben on Cleverbot, he's not responding. I just get the AI.

3:51pm - My ears aren't fooling me, I'm hearing the reverse Song of Healing. I keep hearing it.

4:23pm - Now I'm positive of it, earlier I thought it was a weird coincidence, but just now I went to open my window, and three floors down at ground level I saw the old man. I'm completely positive I did. The same guy. He was just staring up at my window, standing in the middle of campus. If any students took notice of him they didn't seem to acknowledge it.

—

That's where my notes end. I fled my room, taking the cartridge with me. I don't want to go into details of what happened, I'll lose my train of thought as I hammer out these last details. It's been roughly two days since then. This is my last summary and service to you, of the final video you guys saw - Matt.wmv.

The last video entry I made, Matt.wmv, began as normal. I was spawned in Clock Town as usual and nothing seemed to be out of place, determined to set things right and play the Oath to Order ontop of the Clock Tower on the 4th day, I prepared myself. I sped up time and got to the final day, making my way to the observatory. As I got up to the telescope room and approached the astromer, he would not let me look into his telescope. He told me that it would be cheating and that I should follow the rules. Despite my repeated efforts, the game would not let me do the 4th day glitch, no matter how hard or what I tried, I tried working around the game and doing the glitch, but it was adament this time. Regardless of if I simply had the illusion of free will in prior games, this time the game became more aggressive than anything I've ever seen. It eventually told me to go to Ikana Canyon, where the game would end and it would stop haunting me, anxious and desperate to end this nightmare I played the song of soaring and ended up there. I was told to check my inventory, that I would find the answers there to end the game. I arrived at Ikana Canyon and saved my progress at the owl statue. As I searched through my inventory, I finally noticed that I was missing a reoccurring song - the Elegy of Emptiness. Obviously once I traveled there and learned the song, I suppose that was the last thing it needed before BEN decided it had had enough fun playing with me. Ben is a manipulator; he tries to fool his victims into security and makes you drop your guard like a Venus fly trap, he ensnares them. I am nothing but a puppet to him, he enjoys seeing what kind of human emotions he can tap into by doing different things.

There are still some things about this whole experience that still don' t make sense, but then again I never was good at figuring out these things and I'm not exactly in the right state of mind to, I'm giving you all the pieces of the puzzle for you to analyze and piece together the missing links.

I am typing these "closing thoughts" on the library computer on campus, and I've emailed myself the notes I have stored on my "infected" computer from the last four days. I'm then going to combine those copy/paste those notes with the "closing/openings" that I've typed here on the safe, public computer into one text document - I'm not taking any chances spreading Ben, I would not wish this horrible torment on anyone and I've made sure to have my bases covered here. I didn't run into any problems with Ben when I was back on my computer trying to email myself the notes - went right under his fucking nose. He has no idea what he just let me do. Had no problems opening the txt document from my "infected" computer in my email, either. I can't describe to you how it feels to finally be able to get the word out in this post. The nightmare ends here.

That said,

Do not download ANY of my videos or anything ABOUT my videos - through a Youtube video/audio ripper, a screengrab, whatever. I don't know how he can spread, but I know that just watching them on youtube/reading my text won't be able to allow him to spread, otherwise he wouldn't have needed my help in the first place, but I STRONGLY recommend you do not take anything you see streaming online onto your own personal computer.

This will be my last posting, I'm putting up on this forum here for the world. If you see any further posts from me, after today's current date - September 12 - and after the current time - 12:08am - DISCREDIT them. It already has proven to me that Ben can access my account/password and manipulate my computer, and like I said I have no idea to what extent it can do this, but know that it will do anything to break free. He is desperate. To ensure your safety, just forget about me. Please.

And obviously this goes without saying, but from here on out do not download ANY images I may have put up, any files, any ANYTHING.

This fifth day will be my last day, I'm going to burn the cartridge and then come back to destroy my laptop.

Again, even though I don't even know you this is sort of bittersweet for me. This semester I really didn't have any friends, or rather, I stopped paying attention to them.

But I suppose that's partially to blame because I am the genius who picked to live in a single, I suppose someone to get ahold of me and save me before I got too immersed into this game would have literally saved my life. However, it proved too much for me, I'm just glad it happened to me and I could get the warning out so that Ben dies here.

Lastly, thank you for taking the time to open this and open yourselves up to me by hearing my story, despite maybe not believing me. You didn't have to do that - really, you shouldn't have. Your support this entire time has kept me going and now I am finally free of this.

Thanks Again,
Jadusable

...You shouldn't have done that, Matt. You shouldn't have done that....

Printed in Great Britain
by Amazon.co.uk, Ltd.,
Marston Gate.